HAY FEVER

Giles Ratcliffe was the last person Alicia expected to see at her step father's funeral. She had loved him eight years ago and he had lied to her then, so he was also the last person she *wanted* to see! But Giles didn't seem to feel the same way about Alicia . . .

Books you will enjoy
by MARY LYONS

PASSIONATE DECEPTION

Harriet hadn't actually expected Jake Lan
caster to appear in person at this demonstra-
tion. But now that he had she could put
another plan into action . . . But neither had
she expected to see him again, and that
meeting was to be a passionate one, something
Harriet hadn't planned on at all!

ESCAPE FROM THE HAREM

The trouble was, Leonie decided, that her
heart would not let her listen to her head
where Badyr was concerned. True, now that
he was Sultan things might be different in
Dhoman, but that did not mean she was
willing to return there with him. Especially
after the way he had ignored her and their
daughter for the past four years!

HAY FEVER

BY
MARY LYONS

MILLS & BOON LIMITED
15-16 BROOK'S MEWS
LONDON W1A 1DR

First published in Great Britain 1987
by Mills & Boon Limited

© Mary Lyons 1987

Australian copyright 1987
Philippine copyright 1987
This edition 1987

ISBN 0 263 75664 5

Set in Linotron Times 10 on 10 pt.
01-0587-58487

Typeset in Great Britain by
Associated Publishing Services
Printed and bound in Great Britain by
Collins, Glasgow

CHAPTER ONE

'I'M leaving, and I'll never come back—never!'

Alicia sighed, her lips tightening in a rueful grimace as she recalled the last, bitter confrontation with her stepfather. Jed's scornful, derisory laughter at her vow to leave Eastdale and the farm had provoked her beyond all reason and control. 'I swear I'll never come back—*not until you're dead and gone!*' she had cried. The childishly defiant words, uttered with such passion and conviction all those years ago, now echoed with haunting irony in Alicia's head as the large black limousine made its slow progress through the tortuous bends of the icy country roads.

Ever since they had left the motorway, she had become aware of ever-increasing feelings of disquiet and unease. It couldn't be the weather that was causing her to feel so apprehensive. To anyone born and bred in Shropshire, the bleak winter landscape of snow-covered fields beneath a grey sky, heavy with the promise of yet another snow storm, was only too familiar. Maybe it was that very familiarity, the sense of coming home, which was so disturbing? She sighed again, leaning her head back against the seat as she tried to keep the unhappy memories of the past at bay.

It was far too late to turn back now, of course, but it was clearly a mistake to have listened to Elsie. Why on earth had she allowed herself to be persuaded to return for Jed's funeral—a man she had so disliked and despised while he was alive? She'd been so sure that the brief visit would be a relatively unimportant episode in her life. After all, it was eight years since she had run away to London, and with the security of the new existence she had forged for herself, and the increasing maturity of her twenty-four years, she had been so certain, so supremely confident that she had no need to fear the shades of the past. But now that confidence seemed to be rapidly draining away.

'You're looking a bit pale. Are you sure you're feeling okay?'

Alicia turned her head to smile at the girl sitting beside her. 'Yes, I'm fine. It's just been a longer journey than I expected, that's all.'

'The weather's ghastly, isn't it?' Polly said, looking out of the window. 'What we both need is a strong dose of brandy to keep our spirits up. Whoops! Sorry about the dreadful pun!' she giggled, reaching forward to open the flap of a walnut-veneered cabinet. 'It's a bit tough on poor Simpson, though. His job must be hell—all drive and no drink!' she added, nodding her bright copper-coloured, curly head at the back view of the chauffeur on the other side of the glass partition.

Alicia looked at her doubtfully. 'It's a bit early in the day, isn't it?'

'Nonsense,' Polly said briskly, placing a small silver flask in her hands. 'Funerals are hideously depressing affairs. I remember being absolutely shattered by the ceremony after Father's death, for instance. So, a bit of Dutch courage can only be a good thing—right?'

'You're quite right,' Alicia murmured, sipping the pale, tawny liquid and relaxing as the fiery warmth flowed through her veins.

'There you are, you see? I just knew, *dearest Mama*, that you'd be glad I nagged you into letting me come along today!'

'Idiot! Of course I'm glad of your company.' Alicia smiled at her stepdaughter who, at twenty, was only four years younger than herself. 'But don't say I didn't warn you that it's going to be a very long, cold day. After attending the funeral, I must call and see Elsie, the housekeeper at the farm. We can't expect much in the way of lunch, so you're likely to be very tired—not to say hungry!—by the time we get back to London tonight. Quite honestly, I can't think why you wanted to come.'

'Oh, for lots of reasons. Mostly because I've been feeling bored to death lately, I expect.' Polly hesitated for a moment. 'But I must admit to a certain fascination in learning more about your murky past.'

'My what . . .?' Alicia looked at her in astonishment. 'Why this sudden interest? You've known me since I was seventeen, so I really don't see how that gives me much time for a "past"—murky or otherwise!'

'Who said anything about a sudden interest? I've always been intrigued . . . I mean, I've always wondered where you came from, or what you did before you married Father.' Polly grinned sheepishly. 'I know it sounds mad, but when I was younger, I used to have tremendous fantasies about your past. But whenever I brought up the subject, you used to clam up tight like the proverbial oyster, or else quickly change the subject.'

'What nonsense!'

'Oh no, it's not, Ally. For instance, if I hadn't taken that phone call from your old housekeeper—with the news about your stepfather's death—I bet you'd never have told me that you used to live on a farm in Shropshire?'

Alicia gave a dismissive shrug. 'I really can't see that there's anything very exciting or extraordinary about growing up on a farm in the country. If I haven't talked about Winterfloods . . .'

'Winterfloods? Is that the name of your farm?'

'Yes.'

'There you are, you see? I didn't even know that!'

'Honestly, Polly—if I haven't talked about it, it's because . . .' Alicia hesitated, annoyed to feel her

cheeks flushing beneath the amused, quizzical expression on her stepdaughter's freckled face. 'Okay, the
facts are very simple: after my mother's death, I
didn't get on with my stepfather, and when I fell in
love with the wrong man, we had a bad quarrel and I
ran away to work in London. It's a very boring story,
I'm afraid, and since it happened eight years ago, it's
nothing but ancient history now.'

'Hmm . . .' Polly was very sure that there was a lot
more to the story. However, Alicia wasn't going to
enlighten her any further at the moment, she realised,
looking at the finely boned, classical profile of the
beautiful blonde woman who had averted her head to
stare out at the passing scenery.

Alicia's appearance into Polly's lonely, unhappy
childhood had been nothing short of dramatic; a
miraculous answer to her prayers. Looked after by a
succession of various servants, Polly had hardly seen
anything of her elderly father, a wealthy tycoon who
had buried himself in his business affairs after his
wife's death. Sir Walter Preston hadn't deliberately
neglected his thirteen-year-old daughter, but he had
been so immersed with the intricacies of high finance
that he had little or no time for anything else.

Until the day that Polly, carelessly and mindlessly
crossing a busy road, had been saved from almost
certain death by Alicia. Shouting a warning, and
leaping forward to pull the young girl away from the
wheels of a speeding bus, Alicia had been tossed into
the air like a rag doll. Most of her limbs had been
broken, and when she was well enough to be allowed
out of the private hospital, whose astronomical fees
had been paid by Sir Walter, he had also insisted that
Alicia must come to stay at his house in Belgravia
with a professional nurse in attendance, until she was
fully recovered—a decision that had effectively
changed all their lives.

Polly found, in the girl who was only four years
older than herself, a friend, companion and also,

when her father married Alicia a year later, a loving stepmother. There had been much cynical newspaper speculation when it became known than Sir Walter, the hard-headed financier, had taken a beautiful eighteen-year-old girl for his second wife. Polly had been too young to be aware of the gossip about her father's 'child bride'. She had only known that the large house, once so dark and gloomy, had become a haven of warmth and comfort, and that when Sir Walter had died of a heart attack a year ago, it was mainly due to Alicia that his final years had been so happy and content.

Her thoughts were interrupted as Alicia leant forward to give Simpson directions. Looking out of the window, Polly saw that the Rolls was now moving slowly down a wide village street, the shops and houses all appearing to be constructed from the same pale grey stone.

'Is this where you used to live?' she asked, looking about her with interest.

'Yes, this is Eastdale,' Alicia said as the vehicle came to a halt behind some large black cars outside a church. Simpson got out to walk around and open her door, the chauffeur placing a solicitous hand beneath her elbow as she stepped out on to the slippery pavement.

Alicia stood still for a moment, her gaze travelling over the ancient church and on down the village street. Nothing had changed: the Elizabethan school building with its ancient whipping post, the old petrol pump still leaning at a drunken angle outside the tin-roofed garage, the rambling ivy masking the upper windows of the Wheatsheaf Inn; they all appeared to be exactly the same as when she had left the village eight years ago.

'Will you be long, madam?' asked Simpson.

'No,' she murmured, looking over at the small collection of dark-suited figures standing in a far, windswept corner of the graveyard. 'It looks as if the

service is almost over,' she added as Polly got out of
the car and came over to stand shivering beside her.
'Why don't you and Simpson go and keep warm in
the Wheatsheaf? They always used to have a blazing
fire in the winter, and I'll be along to join you just as
soon as I can.'

'I must admit that the thought of a warm fire is
very tempting,' Polly said, pulling up the collar of her
coat against the biting wind. 'Are you sure . . .?'

'Quite sure. There's absolutely no point in us all
catching cold,' Alicia said firmly.

The first few flakes of snow were beginning to fall
as Alicia made her way through the lich-gate and on
down the path, coming to a halt beside a large yew
tree some yards from where the burial service was
being conducted. One by one, the group of people
turned to stare at the stranger in their midst.
Fashionably and expensively clothed against the cold
February morning, her hands were hidden inside a
fur muff which matched the full-length, black mink
coat, over long slender legs terminating in delicate
high-heeled shoes.

The first blank curiosity of the mourners quickly
gave way to a ripple of whispered recognition. There
could be no mistaking that finely boned, oval-shaped
face, strangely mysterious beneath the veil attached
to a small black silk hat, worn at a provocative angle
over the wide sky-blue eyes. Neither had they
forgotten the distinctive ash-blonde hair—which once
had been a cloud of long, tangled waves, but was
now drawn off her face and twisted into a silky-
smooth chignon at the base of her neck.

Oblivious of the furtive glances, and of the low
buzz of excitement engendered by her unexpected
appearance, Alicia's eyes were slowly and inexorably
drawn towards the man standing slightly apart from
the group beside the freshly dug grave.

She felt suddenly faint, as though she had been hit
by a violent blow to the solar plexus, aware of the

blood draining from her face at the sight of the tall, broad-shouldered figure—the tanned, arrogant features of the very last man in the world she expected to see. Almost reeling under the impact of the hard grey eyes which were staring at her with such intensity, Alicia struggled to regain her composure.

What was he doing here? She had been so certain that he wouldn't attend the funeral. Knowing how much Giles Ratcliffe and Jed, her stepfather, had always detested each other, she could have sworn that there wasn't the remotest possibility of meeting him during her brief visit. And now? What on earth was she to do now?

Alicia's facial muscles ached as she strove to maintain an expression of cool, calm uninterest. As the service began to draw to a close, she turned to walk slowly away, almost physically aware of Giles' hard, penetrating eyes following her progress. Rounding the corner, and out of sight of the mourners, she moved as swiftly as she could across the icy path towards the sanctuary of the church.

Choosing a pew that was partly hidden behind a large pillar, she sank weakly to her knees and stared blindly at the flickering lights of the candles on the altar. This was ridiculous! She really must pull herself together. Running away was a childish response, and wasn't going to solve anything. Naturally it had been a shock to see Giles again. And goodness knows she wouldn't have come to the funeral if she had known he was going to be there. But she had, and he was, so she'd better decide what she was going to do about the situation. And quickly! she told herself as she heard the Rector going into the vestry to disrobe.

Deciding to wait for a few minutes, by which time the mourners would have left the graveyard, she gazed up at a memorial tablet on the wall beside her. One of many such commemorative plaques to be seen in the ancient church, its pious verse recorded the passing of a member of the Ratcliffe family, who had been the biggest landowners in the district—and Lords of the Manor of Eastdale—since medieval times.

Of course! So *that* was why Giles was at the funeral. She could have kicked herself, several times over, for not having realised that he was bound to be present at the interment of one of his tenant farmers. The local squirearchy undoubtedly still had a stranglehold on remote country areas such as Eastdale—*noblesse oblige*, and all that rubbish, she thought grimly, rising to her feet and stamping her frozen feet. She was a fool to have let Elsie persuade her into coming back—and the sooner she returned to London, the better.

Waiting until the Rector had left, Alicia emerged from the church to find, as she had hoped, that the graveyard was deserted. The snow was falling even faster now and, shivering with cold, she paused beneath the arch of the church porch, clutching the fur coat more closely about her slim figure.

'Well, well! The prodigal daughter has returned at last, I see!'

The deep, mocking voice had seemed to come from just behind her, and she whirled round, her heart thudding with apprehension and alarm.

'G-Giles . . .?' she whispered, her eyes searching the dim interior of the large porch.

'Who else?' An ironic laugh was followed by the tall figure of Giles, materialising from the dark shadows like some ghostly apparition. 'You wouldn't have been trying to avoid me, would you, Alicia?'

'No—no, of course not.'

The lie rose quickly to her lips as she glanced nervously up at the man who was now towering over her. Not only was she acutely conscious of the threatening width of his broad shoulders, but their close proximity to each other was having the most unnerving effect upon her. Was it his physical

presence, or the long forgotten shades of the past,
which were causing her to be so intensely aware of
the hard-muscled, powerful chest beneath the dark
formal suit, the lean hips and the long length of his
legs? Momentarily confused, she was dismayed to
find that she had allowed herself to be led back into
the shelter of the dimly lit porch.

'I'm afraid I really must go . . .' she muttered,
casually trying to edge away from the hand holding
her arm.

'Must you, really?' he drawled, his lips twisting
with amusement and his grip tightening as he observed
her evasive action.

'Yes, I . . . I only came back . . .' she hesitated.
What on earth was she to say, when even she wasn't
entirely sure why she was here?

'Why have you come back? Was it just curiosity?
Or was it to dance on Jed's grave?'

'No . . .!' She looked up at him in horror. 'That—
that's a despicable . . . a terrible thing to say!'

Giles shrugged. 'I don't see why. I might agree that
such an action isn't exactly in the best of taste.
However, when I heard you were expected to attend
the funeral, and knowing that there was no love lost
between you and Jed . . .'

'Who told you that I was coming?' she demanded
angrily. 'Was it Elsie?'

Giles laughed and shook his head. 'Oh, Alicia, you
can't possibly have forgotten that much about life in
the country. Surely you must remember Mrs Jenkins
at the corner shop? I've always thought that she's
wasted here in Eastdale—she should have placed her
considerable talents at the disposal of MI5 and the
CIA!'

'Yes, well . . .' she shivered as a sudden gust of
wind and snow swept in through the open arch.

'Whatever possessed you to wear such unsuitable
shoes on a day like this?' he said roughly, drawing
her further back into the porch.

'It wasn't particularly cold in London,' she murmured, glancing around uneasily. The falling snow hung like an opaque curtain in the entrance, causing the poorly lit, dark shadowy interior of the enclosed space to take on a curiously intimate atmosphere.

'So . . . you've done your duty and attended Jed's funeral—what now?' he asked, putting his other hand on her shoulder and turning her to face him, his hard grey eyes studying her with an inscrutable expression.

'Giles, I . . .' She cleared her throat nervously as she stared up at the face so close to her own. He really hasn't changed, she thought distractedly. Maybe there were some silver threads beginning to show amid the thick dark hair, a few more lines on the arrogant face, but other than that, Giles was clearly still the same hard, tough personality he had always been.

'What are you *really* doing here?' The voice cutting into her confused, chaotic thoughts was now softer, containing a warmer note so evocative of the distant past that she felt almost faint and dizzy.

Giles looked down at the fluttering dark lashes beneath the delicate veil, the pale cheeks and tremulous lips. With a fierce, sudden intake of breath, his fingers tightened, biting through the fur into her flesh as his mouth stiffened into a hard, straight line.

'Well? I'm still waiting for an answer!' he said tersely. 'Your sudden appearance after what—eight years?—does seem a little odd, to say the least. I can't help wondering why the rich and glamorous widow, Lady Preston, has suddenly decided to be so condescending as to pay us country yokels a visit?'

Alicia gasped at the harsh, sarcastic words, which broke through her emotional disorientation like a jet of cold water. Taking a deep breath and gritting her teeth, she struggled to suppress an overwhelming urge to slap the grim, sardonic smile off his face. What God-given right did he think he had to talk to her like that? He, who had been mainly responsible for so much misery and unhappiness in her life? If it hadn't been for him . . . But that was in the past, she reminded herself quickly. She was now light years away from the over-intense, emotionally starved teenager that he had once known.

'Kindly take your hands off me,' she said icily. 'It's none of your business what I do, or where I go.'

Giles became suddenly still, his face pale and strained as he stared blankly down into her angry blue eyes. When he made no attempt to release her, she quickly twisted herself away and moved swiftly over the flagstones towards the outer arch of the porch. The snow was falling in melting flakes on to the dark fur of her coat as she hesitated, turning to face his tall, rigid figure.

'Ah, but you see you *are* my business, Alicia,' he said, walking slowly over to lean against the carved stone arch, tilting his head to one side as he surveyed her with a cold, grim expression.

'Oh, no, I most certainly am not!' she retorted quickly.

He shrugged his shoulders. 'I would have thought it was obvious that I must take a decision about the tenancy of Winterfloods Farm. As you are the sole surviving member of your family, and undoubtedly an executor of Jed's estate, that must mean discussion of various matters between myself and your business advisers.'

'I . . . I hadn't thought about that,' she muttered.

'Obviously!' His voice was heavy with contempt, and Alicia's cheeks burned as she realised that she had very nearly made a fool of herself. She should have known that his only interest in her was that concerned with the affairs of his land holdings. 'However,' he added caustically, 'please don't let me stop you from running away—yet again.'

Before she could think of a suitable, stinging retort, she was distracted by the distant shout of her name.

'Oh, lord—I quite forgot. That must be Polly . . . I have to go . . .'

'Polly . . .?' He raised a dark eyebrow. 'Got a parrot in that damn big Rolls, have you?'

'Oh, for heaven's sake—don't be so juvenile!' Alicia glared belligerently at Giles. 'Polly Preston is my stepdaughter. She's a very nice girl of whom I'm extremely fond. So, you can just cut out the feeble jokes, okay?'

Giles scowled, thrusting his hands into his pockets, and looking like a man who was only just hanging on to his temper. 'I'm sorry,' he said at last through gritted teeth.

'I should hope so,' she retorted. Being ten years older than her, Giles had always—mentally and physically—had the upper hand. But now, after all these years, Alicia felt quite confident of her ability to stand up to him. She knew that she was probably behaving badly, but nevertheless it was giving her considerable pleasure and satisfaction to be able to release some of the pent-up, burning resentment against this man which she had harboured for so long.

'It's not very important . . . just a minor point, really,' she added casually. 'But since we seem to be on the subject of family relatives—and just to satisfy my idle curiosity, of course—am I correct in assuming that you did marry Camilla? Or were you, in fact, two-timing her as well as myself?'

'My God! You've really turned out to be quite a bitch, haven't you?' he hissed through clenched teeth, a muscle beating wildly in his jaw. 'Oh, yes, I married Camilla—*indeed I did!*'

Alicia flinched at the raw savagery in his voice as he spun on his heels and strode swiftly away, his tall figure soon lost to view in the white blanket of falling snow.

'I hope you didn't mind us coming to fetch you,' Polly said as Alicia climbed in through the door of the Rolls. 'It was lovely and warm in the pub, but when it began filling up with the locals—who kept looking at Simpson and myself as if we were creatures from another planet!—we decided to make ourselves scarce.'

'No . . . yes . . . I mean, I should have thought of that,' Alicia muttered, trying to concentrate on brushing the wet, melting snow off her coat, and striving to banish the disastrous meeting with Giles from her mind. 'Oh, lord, just look at my shoes,' she said, frowning down at the delicate strips of black patent leather as she wriggled her frozen toes. 'I was an absolute fool to have worn them on a day like this.'

'They're certainly not ideal for standing around in the snow,' Polly agreed. 'You must be frozen. Oh, by the way, who was that up-market, Clint Eastwood-type figure who came storming out of the graveyard just now?'

'That . . . that was the local squire,' said Alicia grimly as she reached up to take off her hat.

Polly laughed. 'How incredibly feudal! You should have seen the way he glared at us—if looks could kill, Simpson and I would be dead by now! I can see that he's obviously perfect typecasting as the wicked "Sir Jasper" of this village. I bet he goes around grinding the faces of the poor, not to mention seducing all the innocent young virgins and . . .'

'Oh, do shut up, Polly!' Alicia snapped.

Her stepdaughter looked at her with startled eyes. It wasn't like Alicia to be so irritable. She must have been upset by the funeral, although now, as she gave Polly an apologetic smile before instructing Simpson on how to find Winterfloods Farm, she appeared to be her normal, calm self once more.

'What a marvellous name for a farm.' Polly's bright green eyes sparkled with interest, quickly forgetting Alicia's brief flash of bad temper, as the car left the village street and, rounding a corner, moved slowly on down a small country lane. It was all so silent, just the crunching sound of the wheels on packed snow and an occasional bird to be seen on the icy white branches of the trees. 'Has your family lived there for a long time?'

'I believe my father's family, the Howards, have been farming here since the beginning of the eighteen-hundreds. They passed it down from father to son, so I suppose that it's sad now, that as an only daughter with no other relatives, I'm the end of the line.'

'What are you going to do with . . . *Oh, Alicia!*' Polly gasped as they rounded a corner. 'It's fantastic! What a lovely place—how could you ever bear to leave it?'

Passing over a cattle grid set between two stone gateposts, the Rolls drew up outside a rambling, black and white-timbered house. Snugly enfolded by giant oak trees, whose bare branches were heavy with snow, the farmhouse and its setting would have provided a perfect illustration for a Dickensian Christmas card.

Polly opened her door, jumping out to view the chimneys rising like twisted barley-sugar canes from the long, uneven line of the old sandstone-tiled roof. The diamond-shaped panes of glass set within the leaded windows were surrounded by elaborately carved heavy black beams, which formed complicated and intricate patterns over the white plasterwork. It was a quite unique and rare example of an Elizabethan farmhouse, which had been virtually untouched since the day it was built; a remarkable survival from a more individual and less uniform age.

'It's so . . . so . . .' Polly gestured with excitement as she hunted for a word to express her delight.

'. . . so cold in the winter,' Alicia said drily as she came to stand beside her stepdaughter. 'I agree that, yes, it's very beautiful, but when you've lived in it for some time, I think you'd find yourself wishing for just

a little central heating and a few modern comforts—
such as an efficient plumbing system, for instance.'

'Philistine!' Polly laughed. 'Honestly, I don't think
that you've got a romantic bone in your body.'

If I ever had, I must have lost it years ago, Alicia
thought, looking up at the house which held so many
unhappy memories for her. She was filled with an
extraordinary mixture of sensations, none of which
she quite understood or wished to explore at the
moment, and was therefore grateful to see the heavy
oak front door open. The woman who appeared in
the doorway was a round, squat figure who stood on
the threshold with arms akimbo, surveying the new
arrivals with ferocious little boot-button eyes.

'Come along, Miss Alicia,' she barked. 'I've got
more to do than stand here all day! And if you think
I'm going to have my steak and kidney pie spoilt,
waiting for folks who should by rights have been here
long ago, you've got another think coming!'

Polly looked on apprehensively as Alicia ran
forward and threw her arms around the small, fierce
little woman.

'Oh, Elsie,' she murmured, kissing the older
woman's hard red cheeks. 'How I've missed you! It's
been such a long time, and . . .'

'There now, that's quite enough of that nonsense,'
Elsie Wade said sharply, brushing what looked
suspiciously like a tear from her eye. 'You come
along in and get warm,' she said, leading the way
through the oak-panelled hall and on down a
flagstoned corridor to the kitchen.

The kitchen was a large room, filled with the
delectable smell of new bread, which was cooling on
an oak dresser, and the aroma of a freshly baked
beef pie. The windows were covered with faded red
and white checked curtains, and the red-tiled floor
was covered with bright rugs. In front of the Aga
stove was an old-fashioned fender of polished brass,
and lying beside it was an elderly black and white

sheepdog, who sat up and thumped its tail as they
entered the room.

'Come along and take off that fancy coat,' Elsie
commanded, sweeping a large tabby cat off a chair
before she turned to survey Alicia's companions.
'And who might these folk be?'

'This is my stepdaughter, Polly Preston,' Alicia
said, 'and we've been driven here by Simpson. I
think it might be a good idea to put the car under
cover somewhere, but . . .'

'You just leave the car and Mr Simpson to me,'
said Elsie, firmly pushing the two younger women out
into the hall. 'He can have his lunch in the old
scullery—it's nice and warm there by the boiler. Go
and wash your hands and have a sherry, and I'll have
your meal ready in two ticks.'

'Elsie's a bit . . . well, she's a bit fierce, isn't she?'
Polly remarked as Alicia led her into a large sitting-
room, whose walls were panelled with the same
honey-coloured oak as in the hall.

'No, she's not,' Alicia smiled as she walked across
to where logs were blazing in the wide ingle-nook
fireplace. 'The truth is that Elsie's an old softy, whose
bark is far worse than her bite. I've known her all my
life, and when I left she was the only person with
whom I ever kept in touch.'

'Why did you leave?' Polly asked, bending down to
warm her hands at the fire.

'Oh, lots of reasons,' Alicia murmured evasively,
looking around at the shabby, torn furnishings on the
chairs and sofas. 'When my parents were alive, this
used to be a lovely room—and now look at it! Jed
would have been quite happy living in a pigsty,' she
added curtly. 'He was only interested in the land, but
it's almost criminal the way he's neglected the house
and allowed it to deteriorate like this.'

'I'm getting a bit confused,' Polly said. 'This Jed
person, whose funeral you went to today: he was
married to your mother—right?'

'Yes.'

'But what happened to your real father?'

Alicia sighed, and sat down on a stool by the fire. 'It's very simple, really. My father, John Howard, died very suddenly of cancer when I was eleven and, as you can imagine, it was quite a struggle for my mother to keep the farm going on her own. I helped in the school holidays, of course, but it soon became too much for her to cope with. So she engaged a man, Jed Black, as farm manager.' She paused, staring into the fire. 'Well, one thing led to another, and a year later he and my mother got married. Jed, who came from Yorkshire, was a man of few words and little or no interest in anything but farming. He and I . . . well, we never got on, and after my mother died two years later, it became a case of open warfare between us. So, I eventually left and went to look for a job in London. End of story.'

She tilted her head as she heard a call from the kitchen. 'It sounds as though our lunch is ready. I warn you that Elsie will take it as a personal insult if you don't eat up every scrap—which won't be too hard, because she's a brilliant cook.'

'My God, this is wonderful!' Polly mumbled some time later, her mouth full of succulent beef and melting pastry. 'Can I have a second helping?'

'I do likes to see a young girl enjoying her food; it's a rare old sight these days, I can tell you.' Elsie beamed at Polly's rounded curves. 'Not like your stepma, here. And what have you been a-doing of yourself, I'd like to know?' she demanded, pausing from her bustle around the kitchen to glare at Alicia. 'You looks terrible. It's not right to be so thin. If you're not careful, you'll have lost all your beauty by the time you're thirty. London, indeed! And a fine time it's been for me, worrying myself sick about you a-living so far away.'

'Don't scold me, Elsie,' Alicia said gently as the older woman paused to draw breath. 'When you're young, and unhappy, you don't always stop to think about other people.'

'Hmm. Well, least said soonest mended, so I'd best change the subject, I suppose,' she muttered, banging down a saucepan. 'Was there a good turn out for the funeral?'

'There seemed to be quite a few people, but I didn't have time to meet them since we arrived rather late.'

'Was Squire there?' Elsie asked casually as she placed another large helping of steak and kidney on Polly's plate.

'Yes.'

'Talk to him, did you?'

'We did . . . er . . . have a few, brief words.'

'Ah . . . I thought it likely that you might!'

Polly had been following the cryptic, over-casual conversation with some interest. 'This Squire that you mention—was he the tall, dark chap who rushed out of the churchyard in such a rage?'

'Angry, was he?' asked Elsie as Alicia ignored the question, bending down to stroke the black and white sheepdog, who had come over to place its head on her lap.

'He looked furious!' Polly grinned. 'Mind you, he's obviously very good-looking—in a grim sort of way. Is he always so bad-tempered?'

'Oh, dear me, no. Mr Ratcliffe was always such a fine, upstanding man, until . . . but there, I'm not one who's given to idle tittle-tattle, you know. Not like some I could mention, such as that Mrs Jenkins at the corner shop,' Elsie added darkly.

'Of course not,' Polly agreed, trying to keep her face straight as the older woman pulled up a chair, clearly intending to settle down for a good gossip.

'Well . . . I don't suppose there's any harm in telling you what's only the truth . . .'

'Mmm . . .?' Polly murmured encouragement.

Elsie shook her head sorrowfully, leaning forward

as she lowered her voice. 'Goodness knows that poor man has had his share of troubles. And, you wouldn't believe what that wife of his . . .'

'That was a wonderful meal,' Alicia interrupted quickly. 'And it's been lovely to see you again, Elsie, but I'm afraid that we'll have to be on our way very soon.'

Elsie looked up. 'You might wants to be on your way, Miss Alicia, but I don't rightly see as how you can leave just yet.'

'Oh, Elsie, you know I'd like to stay a bit longer . . .'

'Like to or not—I reckon you'll have to,' said Elsie flatly. 'My Fred, what does the cattle and sheep, has been took to his bed for these past two days. He has the 'flu something shocking, and the doctor says he must stay a-bed for the next week at least. There's sheep in the paddock ready for lambing, and the calves and heifers need feeding regular, too. So who's going to do the work, that's what I'd like to know?'

'But there must be someone!' Alicia protested. 'Who's been looking after the stock since Jed died?'

'Fred did what he could, but he were already sickening for the 'flu. So, he sees the Squire, who asked Mr Barlow—him what has Raven's Farm—if he could spare his boy. The lad was a good worker, but they're lambing up at Ravens now, and he can't come no more. All the farms is busy with lambing, and there's no men to spare.' Elsie shrugged her shoulders. 'Besides, just afore you come back from the funeral, I had a telephone call from that there Mr Pemberton, him what was the lawyer for your father and mother. It seems he wants to see you tomorrow, about Jed's will, he said. So you might want to get back to London, but I don't reckon you've got any choice other than to stay here, my girl.'

Alicia groaned. 'But we can't possibly do that.'

'Oh yes, we can, Ally!' said Polly excitedly. 'I'll help you feed the animals, and do whatever has to be done. I'm sure we can manage, and it will be so much more fun than trotting off back to London. Do let's stay!'

'Oh, for heaven's sake, Polly, you've no idea of the amount of work involved,' Alicia retorted, putting a hand to her forehead for a moment as she desperately tried to think what to do. Having been away for so many years, she was completely out of touch with the rest of the farming community in the area. If Elsie was right, and everyone was busy seeing to their sheep at lambing time, then it looked as if she might have to stay on here for a few days—unless she could find someone to look after the farm.

Cudgel her brains as she might, she kept coming back to the same conclusion. That there was only one person who might be able to find a man to take on the work immediately, and although she loathed and detested the idea of having to speak to him again, she didn't see that she had any choice.

A few minutes later she was sitting at a desk in the farm office, her fingers shaking nervously as she dialled the number of Eastdale Hall. What on earth was she going to say if Camilla answered her call? Maybe it would be better to try and cope with the work on the farm? Surely *anything* would be better than having to go cap in hand to the man with whom she had had such a furious row only a few hours ago. She hesitated, the decision being taken out of her hands as Giles answered the phone.

Haltingly, she explained the problem. '. . . so, I wondered if you could possibly think of anyone who can help me?'

'I'm afraid I can't, Alicia. It looks as if you're stuck here in Eastdale for the time being,' he said, the sardonic amusement in his deep voice quite apparent, even over the phone. 'Oh, by the way, I do hope that you've brought some other clothes with you. I don't think that mucking out the cowsheds in that very glamorous fur coat is going to do it any good at all, do you?'

'Thank you—for absolutely *nothing*!' she snapped, slamming down the receiver on the sound of his mocking laughter.

CHAPTER TWO

ALICIA stood staring blindly out of the window at the grey stone farm buildings. It was foolish to have lost her temper just now. Slamming the phone down hadn't achieved anything, other than to relieve her exasperated feelings, of course. In fact, considering how helpful Giles had been after Jed's death, by arranging for someone to help Elsie's husband, Fred, with the animals, she ought to have tried to control her temper, even if she couldn't bring herself to express her gratitude. However, it was now certain that Giles wouldn't offer any help in the future—her phone call had seen to that! Why on earth couldn't she have ignored his snide remarks, and played the role of a poor, helpless widow?

Despite all her problems, Alicia couldn't help smiling wryly at the thought of trying to portray herself as a pathetic, forlorn little woman. Giles wasn't likely to be taken in by such a performance. Having known her all his life, he would be well aware that she had been brought up to cope with all the hard work necessary on a farm. Besides, the idea of crawling to him for help was definitely more than she could stomach. Which brought her straight back to square one: what on earth was she going to do now?'

Turning to look around the small room which served as a farm office, she wrinkled her nose in disgust at the piles of dusty papers and magazines covering every available surface. She could remember how different it had been when her father had been alive. During the winter, there was always a cheery fire in the grate, and in summer a bowl of flowers on the ordered, tidy desk. If she had to stay on at the farm, and it very much looked as if she was going to have to remain here for a few days, then it would give her considerable pleasure to make sure that this office had a good spring clean—if only to remove all trace of Jed's occupation.

She leant forward to switch on the desk lamp. The low wattage of the light bulb didn't entirely succeed in banishing all the late afternoon shadows in the small room, but at least it did go some way to relieving the dark, dour shades of Jed's personality which she could feel all around her. Turning back to stare out at the falling snow, Alicia concentrated on trying to prevent her mind from sliding out of control. Over the years, she had learnt to ignore the past, teaching herself to discipline her thoughts and to erase all hurtful memories. She was well aware of the current views of fashionable psychiatrists, much given to pontificating on television that the way to true happiness, and a healthy mind, was to relive past miseries. It was not an opinion with which she concurred. She had always thought of herself as an ordinary, rational human being who chose not to think too much, or dwell too long on the unhappiness of her life with Jed.

She shivered as the damp, chilly tentacles of the past seemed to ooze their way about her still figure. Maybe if she hadn't objected so strongly to her mother's marriage to Jed, events might have turned out differently, but she doubted it. Their personalities had clashed from the moment they had set eyes on each other, and although she could now see that he had tried, as best he could, to make friends with his rebellious young stepdaughter, Alicia had bitterly resented anyone taking her father's place, and hadn't been prepared to give one inch. They had managed to co-exist uneasily together while her mother was alive, the older woman making sure that the mutual antagonism and antipathy between Jed and Alicia never flared up out of control. However, her mother's death when Alicia was only fourteen had been the catalyst for all that followed.

Desperately missing her mother's loving warmth and companionship, Alicia had taken all her unhappiness out on Jed, becoming wild and disobedient. That, together with her repeated accusations that he had been the cause of her mother's death, had led Jed to react with baffled rage at his inability to deal with what had seemed an intractable problem. Left alone with a stepdaughter who was deliberately rude and almost ungovernable, he had been unable to cope with the situation, becoming increasingly cold and withdrawn, and ignoring her existence as far as possible.

Looking back down the years, Alicia could now see that she had been at least half to blame for the situation. But, being so young, she had only been aware of her own deep misery, and desperately in need of love and understanding. And so the matter had continued for two long years, until one June evening, when she was sixteen, she had met and fallen head over heels in love with Giles Ratcliffe . . .

There's absolutely no point in thinking about *that*, she told herself roughly, leaning her hot cheek against the frozen window pane. It was only her quite unexpected meeting with Giles at the funeral, and being forced to stay on here at Winterfloods, which was responsible for her somewhat overwrought state. All she had to do was to find someone to run the farm, and then she could go back to London and her safe, ordered existence. Walter Preston had given her the precious gift of five years of marriage which, if they had been lacking in emotional intensity, had nevertheless been years of quiet happiness and contentment. It was a gift she did not intend to squander. Squaring her shoulders and resolutely taking a deep breath, Alicia switched off the light and left the room.

Entering the kitchen, she found that Elsie had finished the washing-up and was chatting to Polly, who was now sitting on the fender by the Aga and making friends with Jed's old sheepdog.

'It may be my imagination, but I'm sure that the snow seems to be falling faster now,' Alicia said, gratefully accepting the cup of coffee which had been kept warm on the stove.

'That it is,' Elise agreed. 'And likely to get worse, I reckon.'

'Well, I'm afraid that it looks as if I'll have to stay on here at the farm, for the time being anyway.' Alicia sighed and sipped her coffee. 'However, there's absolutely no point in hanging on to the Rolls—it's hardly the ideal transport for a sick sheep, for instance!—and so I think I'd better send Simpson back to London this afternoon, while the roads around here are still passable. And I want you to go with him, Polly,' she added.

'Oh, come on, Ally, don't be so beastly!' the younger girl protested. 'Why should you have all the fun? I'm dying to stay on up here, and you can't possibly do all the work on your own, you know you can't!'

'Hang on! I'm not suggesting that you can't stay here, I'm only asking you to go back with Simpson. And if you'd just calm down for a minute, I'll tell you why.'

Polly grimaced. 'Okay, I'm listening, but it had better be a good reason, that's all.'

'Don't be such an idiot—the answer is staring you in the face. I mean, just look at me.' Alicia glanced down at her slim black wool dress. 'I can't possibly work on the farm dressed like this, and as for these shoes . . .' She pointed a toe at the girl. 'Not exactly perfect footwear for mucking out the cows, now are they? And your clothes aren't much better.'

'Your stepma's quite right,' Elsie said, looking at Polly's fully gathered, three-quarter-length navy-blue skirt over high-heeled boots, topped by a high-necked white cotton blouse. 'You look right fancy, my girl, but them clothes and that long cashmere sweater you was a-wearing earlier—well, they won't last more'n five minutes in that there cow shed. That I do know!'

'That's why you've got to go back to London with Simpson,' Alicia explained. 'We're going to need all the warm clothes you can lay your hands on—particularly those heavy jumpers we wore when we went skiing last year. I can get woollen gloves, heavy cord trousers and Wellington boots up here. But if this snow keeps on falling, we're going to get soaking wet, and that means we must have lots of warm clothes to change into. Okay?'

'Yes, well . . . I suppose so,' Polly muttered. 'But I'm jolly well going to come back tomorrow, so don't try and tell me that I can't!'

Alicia grinned. 'I wouldn't dream of it. Believe me, I'm going to be so cold that I'll be counting the hours until you return! You should be able to load everything into your Mini, and I don't think the journey back will be a problem, not until you leave the motorway. All I ask is that you make sure Simpson gives you a good map, and also a spade to dig yourself out of any snow drifts if you should run into trouble.'

However, it soon became clear to Alicia that Polly wasn't going to leave until she had been shown around the farm buildings. After a hunt through the back scullery, they found some old pairs of rubber boots and two mud-spattered waterproof jackets.

Polly noticed that Alicia shuddered slightly as she put on the thick, heavy garment which dwarfed her slim figure. 'Did that coat belong to Jed?' she asked quietly.

'I suppose it must have. I know it sounds silly, but . . .'

'No, it doesn't. I'm sure it's perfectly natural to feel awkward about . . . well, about wearing his things. Especially if you didn't like him. I mean . . . oh, golly, I'm not saying the right thing, am I?'

'It's all right. I'd be a hyprocrite if I pretended that Jed and I ever got on, because we didn't. When you're as young as I was—fourteen or so—everything's either black or white. I saw people as either innocent or evil, without realising that there are so many shades of grey in between.' Alicia paused as she tied a scarf over her hair. 'For years I hated and loathed Jed. I was quite convinced that he had caused my mother's death, for instance. And I don't suppose that my repeatedly accusing him of doing so helped matters.' She sighed heavily. 'It was your father who taught me to understand that Jed was just a dour, unimaginative man, who hadn't the slightest idea of how to cope with an over-intense, over-emotional teenager.'

'Jed sounds dreadful! Did he really cause your mother's death?'

'No, of course not—or only in so far as the fact that he married her in first place.' Alicia gave an unhappy shrug. 'It was just one of those silly, stupid accidents of fate. My mother wasn't in the first flush of youth, and I suppose she must have thought her childbearing days were over. So she didn't realise she was pregnant, and that the baby was unfortunately developing in her Fallopian tube and not the womb. Of course, if she'd been to a pre-natal clinic, it would have been discovered in time. The first she knew about the pregnancy was when the whole thing went disastrously wrong. I was away at school at the time, and when I got home . . . well, it was far too late— she was already dead.'

'Oh, Ally, how awful!'

'Well, it all happened a very long time ago,' Alicia said as she opened the scullery door, leading the way down a short passage and on out to the cobbled farm yard. 'Far more important at the moment is that I've been away for such a long time, that I really haven't a clue where Jed's been keeping the stock, or exactly what he . . . *be careful!*' she cried as Polly slipped on the snow. 'I think we'd better start at this end of the buildings; at least we'll be under shelter,' she added, moving gingerly over a patch of ice.

'Oh, aren't they sweet!' Polly exclaimed as they entered the old stone barn, which had been divided into two sections. 'This lot of cows look younger than those over there,' she said, leaning over some iron railings to stroke the neck of a small black and white animal.

Alicia laughed. 'The first thing you'll have to learn is the correct terminology! Those in this pen are calves—about six months old, I'd say. While the ones over there,' she pointed across the barn, 'they're young Friesian heifers of about eighteen months, who are already in calf from either a bull or the AI man.'

'The AI man? Who's he?'

'AI stands for artificial insemination. The man from the Ministry comes along and injects a bull's semen into the heifer. It's no big deal—and normally only takes about ten seconds.'

'Ugh! That doesn't sound much fun—for the cow, I mean!'

'Well, it may be tough luck on the cow, but it's a lot cheaper than keeping a bull.' Alicia opened the railings and went over to look in the feeding troughs on the far wall. 'It looks as if they've had their concentrates for today, so I'll only need to give them some more hay tonight,' she called out, before moving along to inspect the water tap and red salt lick.

'What's going to happen to the calves and the . . . er . . . heifers?' asked Polly, smiling at the blissful expression on the face of a small calf as she tickled it behind the ears.

'I expect Jed will have bought all these animals when they were just a few days old, feeding and keeping them out in the meadows during the summer and bringing them in here for the winter. When the older heifers are ready, he'd probably take them to the nearest market, or a supplier, and sell them as 'downcalvers'—just a week or two before they have their calves, and start their milking career.'

'I'd love to have a cow of my own,' Polly said, following behind as Alicia closed the iron railing and began to walk towards a door in the far wall of the stone barn.

'Oh, yes?' Alicia gave her a sceptical grin. 'No doubt you've got this idea of yourself, wearing a mob cap and carrying a three-legged stool, hand milking a nice, placid Jersey cow, hmm?'

'Well, yes, I was picturing something rather like that,' Polly grinned sheepishly.

Alicia gave a dry snort of laughter. 'Well, I suppose miracles can happen. But I don't somehow see you getting up at six or seven o'clock every morning, settling down to an hour's hand milking—and repeating the whole thing in the late afternoon—day in and day out, for ten months of the year.

'I'm sorry to have to disillusion you,' she continued, as she pushed open a heavy oak door. 'But, unfortunately, farming isn't the sweet, "let's all get back to nature" type of occupation that some people believe it to be. Most of the time it's sheer damned hard work which has to be carried out in all weathers, and if you've got stock to look after you'll be very lucky if you manage to get a holiday once every five years!'

'I'm sure you're right, but I'd still like to keep a cow,' Polly said stubbornly, looking up at the high, vaulted ceiling of the large barn, and then at the collection of various farm implements and machinery. 'It all looks . . .' she hesitated for a moment. 'Well, everything does look rather old, doesn't it?'

'Yes, most of this stuff is out of date, not to say

obsolete,' Alicia agreed grimly. 'Trust Jed not to spend a penny if he didn't absolutely have to!'

'Is that the tractor that caused the accident?' Polly asked, pointing to an ancient vehicle, leaning drunkenly to one side. 'How did it happen?'

'From what Elsie said, it seems that Jed had brought the sheep down from the hill, and had gone back to fetch the heavy feeding troughs. Maybe all that bouncing over hard ground was too much for the old tractor, but a wheel-shaft sheered off and the vehicle toppled over, killing Jed immediately.' Alicia sighed. 'Maybe if he'd had a cab on the tractor, he might have escaped. But without even a roll bar—and he must have known that it's quite illegal not to have one—he hadn't a hope, I'm afraid.'

Both the girls were feeling rather subdued as they completed their tour of the farm buildings, before making their way slowly through the snow to look at the sheep in a nearby paddock.

'Most of these ewes look as if they're going to have their lambs any minute,' said Alicia gloomily, looking at the barrel-shaped stomachs of the animals as they finished up the last of their morning ration of hay. 'I don't see how I can possibly hope to cope with them out here in this weather, so I think I'd better try and bring them inside the barn tomorrow.'

Three quarters of an hour later, Alicia had waved goodbye to Polly and Simpson on their way back to London, and managed to convince Elsie that she was quite capable of looking after herself.

'It's time you went home. You know what men are like when they're ill, and I expect Fred is bellowing for some attention by now!' she told the older woman. 'I'm not at all worried about staying in the house on my own, and in any case, I've got too much work to do, feeding and watering the animals, to have time to think any morbid thoughts,' she said firmly, sending the housekeeper on her way back to her own cottage.

She hadn't realised just how true her words would

turn out to be, she thought, as she came back into the kitchen after having fed the animals—a task which had taken far longer than she had bargained for.

'You've gone soft, my girl!' she told herself, attempting to ease her aching muscles as she leant up against the hot stove and tried to bring some life back to her frozen fingers. The calves and heifers hadn't been any trouble, but it had been hard work hauling the bales of hay from the barn, across the frozen farmyard and over to the paddock where the sheep were penned. Luckily, she had taken a large torch with her, otherwise she wouldn't have seen that one of the ewes had managed to slip over on to her back, with all four legs straight up in the air. It might have looked a comical sight to anyone not used to sheep, but she knew that if she didn't get the animal back on its feet as quickly as possible, the ewe would soon die from breathing difficulties. She had eventually managed to turn the heavy beast over, with little or no damage that she could see in the darkness, but it was a job that had left her feeling more tired and exhausted than she could have believed possible. What she needed, she decided, was a long soak in a hot bath.

Walking slowly through the cold, empty house, whose ancient timbers were creaking from the inclement weather outside, she was faintly ashamed of herself for switching on every available light to dispel the dark, gloomy atmosphere she could feel pressing on her from every side.

'I don't believe in ghosts!' she declared loudly as she mounted the stairs, her words echoing back from the high vaulted ceiling of the upper landing.

Entering her old bedroom, she went over to sit down on the small four-poster bed in which she had slept since her early childhood, relishing the soft, yielding comfort of its goose feather mattress. Suddenly overcome by nostalgia, she realised that her room hadn't been changed in any way since the day

she had left. It must be Elsie who had cared for the
old oak furniture; only regular polishing could achieve
that deep gleaming finish that shone in the soft light
of her bedside lamp. In fact, now she came to think
of it, none of the rooms upstairs had been touched or
even redecorated. She hadn't been able to face going
into Jed's bedroom, and had offered up a prayer of
thanks to Elsie for clearing away his things from the
bathroom.

With a sigh, she got up and went over to open the
large wardrobe, shaken to discover that her old
clothes of eight years ago were still hanging there,
just as she had left them. They were all hopelessly
out of date now, of course, although she could
perhaps still manage to get into some of the pairs of
faded blue jeans. They, at least, would prove useful
for working around the farm, as would some of the
old threadbare sweaters neatly stacked on the top
shelf.

As she brushed aside an old dress, prior to closing
the wardrobe door, she disturbed some of the small
muslin sachets of pot-pourri attached to the hangers.
Their sweet perfume filled the room, and she was
suddenly transported back to the days when, as a
small girl, she had helped her mother to gather the
red rose petals and the stalks of lavender which were
then carefully dried and mixed with other scented
flowers and herbs, such as lemon verbena and
bergamot, before the final addition of various aromatic
gums and resins. The old family recipe for pot-pourri
had been handed down from her great-grandmother,
and was now an almost forgotten art in these days of
easily available scents and perfumes.

Alicia's aching muscles reminded her of the need
for a bath, and she was just settling down in the hot
water, groaning with pleasures as her frozen limbs
began to thaw at last, when she heard the telephone
ringing. Barely able to repress a thoroughly rude
expression, she would have ignored its strident

summons if she hadn't suddenly realised that it might be Polly. It was too soon for her to have reached London, and Alicia jumped from the bath, hurriedly covering herself with a towel and rushing downstairs as she realised that her stepdaughter and Simpson might have met with an accident.

'Hello . . .?' she said breathlessly as she lifted the receiver.

'Alicia?'

'Who's that speaking?' she demanded, instantly recognising Giles' deep, dark tones, but damned if she was going to acknowledge the fact that she'd know his voice anywhere.

'Oh, come on, Alicia—it's been a long day and I don't feel like playing games,' he sighed heavily. 'Who else is likely to be calling you at this time of night?'

'Any number of people,' she retorted quickly. 'And since you've just hauled me out of a hot bath, could you please say what you've got to say as quickly as possible?'

'I merely called because I understand you're on your own tonight, and . . .'

'Who told you that?'

'God give me patience!' his harsh voice grated in her ear. 'What does it matter who told me? The point is: are any of your ewes lambing and, if they are, do you need any assistance?'

'No, I—I checked the sheep about a hour ago, and they all seemed to be okay.' She paused, nervously tucking a stray coil of hair back up into the knot tied on top of her head. 'It's—well, it's kind of you to be concerned, and I'm—er—sorry that I was rude on the phone this afternoon . . .' Her voice trailed away and there seemed to be a very long silence before he spoken again.

'You're not the only one who needs to apologise,' he said quietly. 'I wasn't in the best of moods myself, earlier today. And when you made that reference to Camilla . . .'

'I'm sorry,' she said quickly. 'I—I do realise that I shouldn't have said what I did. Whatever happened in the past—well, it really isn't important any more, is it? I'm sure she's made you very happy, and . . .'

'If you're trying to be amusing, let me tell you that you certainly aren't succeeding!' he ground out savagely.

'For heaven's sake! What is it with you?' she demanded angrily. 'I was only trying to be polite. Quite frankly, I couldn't care less about you, or your precious wife. And if her temper is anything like yours, then I can only assume that you both fully deserve each other!'

There was a long pause filled by his harsh, heavy breathing. 'You really don't know, do you?'

'Know what?' she snapped angrily.

'That Camilla and I were divorced over five years ago,' he said in a flat, toneless voice.

'No, of course I didn't . . .' she gasped, and then realised, from the sharp click in her ear, that he had put down the phone. Looking blankly at the receiver in her own hand, it was some time before she slowly replaced the instrument.

'How could I possibly have known about his divorce? I didn't even know—not for certain, anyway—that the swine was married!' she muttered angrily to herself, making her way back up the stairs, and shivering as she clutched the damp towel about her slim figure. After all, the whole point in running away from Eastdale had been to put as much distance as possible between herself and her youthful past. She hadn't *wanted* to know anyone or anything which could in any way remind her of either Jed or the deep, searing humiliation she had suffered at Giles' hands. And in fact, other than writing to Elsie once a year at Christmas, when she would also enclose some money to pay for flowers to be placed on her parents' grave, she had virtually succeeded in eliminating her past existence from her present life.

Lowering herself into the hot water once again, Alicia lay back in the old fashioned cast-iron bath and tried to think back over her encounter with Giles earlier in the day. It was now clear to see just how hurtful he must have found her enquiries about Camilla. She had, of course, intended her remarks to be malicious and spiteful, and had only been surprised by the violence of his reaction before he dashed off into the snow. But now she desperately wished that she had known of his divorce. Wanting to lash back at him for the wounds he had inflicted so long ago was perhaps understandable, but she would never have been so deliberately unkind if she had known about his divorce.

Stepping out of the bath and reaching for a fresh towel, she paused as a frown creased her forehead. She had obviously been in the wrong, and equally obviously she'd have to try and make some sort of apology when she next saw Giles. Not that she was likely to see him again, of course, she thought grimly, as she briskly towelled herself dry. It was bound to take him some time to calm down, and probably even longer before he would be able to see that she had made a genuine mistake. By the time that happened— if it ever did—she would have found someone to look after the farm, and returned to her life in London. But it hadn't been all her fault, had it? It could just possibly be her imagination, but she was quite sure that his temper had already been on a very short fuse *before* they had even exchanged a word in the church porch. And why had he been so full of rage, when it was he who had seduced and then deserted her all those years ago?

The question was still occupying her mind some time later as she sat in a chair beside the warm kitchen stove. While she hadn't known of his marital problems, he, for his part, had seemed to be

well informed about her present circumstances. He
appeared to know that she had married Walter, and
that she was now a widow. What had he said?
Something about 'the glamorous Lady Preston'? Well,
he ought to see her now! She almost laughed aloud
as she glanced down at her extrordinary get-up. There
couldn't be many people sitting in their kitchens
tonight, their feet covered by thick woollen socks
stuffed inside high-heeled shoes, and wearing a mink
coat over a thick cotton nightdress which she had
worn as a child. Not exactly *haute couture*—but what
the hell!

She was still smiling at the thought of parading
down Bond Street in her outlandish apparel when
Jed's dog came over to sit down beside her.

'Poor old Rex, you miss your master, don't you?'
she said, stroking his head. Rex had been a young
dog in his prime that last summer she had spent at
the farm. If Jed was away, the sheepdog would often
accompany her as she roamed the countryside. Far
luckier than many town children in such circumstances,
she had been able to escape from Jed by hiding in
the barns or running off into the woods and hills that
ringed the farm. Hidden in the branches of her
favourite oak tree, she had often seen the distant
figure of Giles Ratcliffe riding about his estate, and
the Hall Farm which adjoined the land her family
had farmed for generations. She had, of course,
known him all her life. Much older than she was, he
had not only rescued her from various childish
scrapes, but had often visited her parents when he
was on holiday from boarding school—principally to
gorge himself on her mother's freshly made bread
and butter, topped by delicious honey collected from
the beehives at the end of the garden. Alicia's mother
had felt sorry for Giles. 'The poor boy, losing his
parents in that car crash, and rattling around the Hall
with no company of his own age—it isn't right. The
old Squire should do something, but . . .' and she

would sigh helplessly, it being common knowledge
that the loss of his only son had turned Giles'
grandfather into a morbid, surly old recluse.

Alicia had thought Giles lucky to be able to have
the whole of Eastdale Hall virtually to himself. An
ancient Jacobean mansion, it stood on the remains of
an old Priory, and was rumoured to contain not only
a ghost, but also a secret passage which led to a
nearby ruined chapel. As she grew older, the large
house seemed the very essence of romance, as indeed
did Giles himself, the orphan boy who had been
carelessly kind to her having grown into a tall, dark
and handsome man. Looking back, it was clear to see
that she must have been subconsciously half in love
with him for almost as long as she could remember.
However, it wasn't until that long, hot summer when
she was sixteen that she had become aware of her
own attraction. She had grown to be as tall and leggy
as a young colt, and the village lads had begun to
buzz around her like bees drawn to a honeypot.
Having no one to tell her, she hadn't really understood
why boys she had known all her life, and indeed
some grown-up men, should have been drawn to the
shy, hesitant girl with her wild cloud of wavy ash-
blonde hair, and the brilliant blue eyes set in a face
of classical beauty. Emerging into womanhood, she
had naturally enjoyed the attention, but she had
never really had eyes for anyone else but Giles.
Bitterly at odds with Jed, who saw her only as a
source of cheap labour about the farm, and emotionally
starved of love and kindness, it was no wonder that
she had invested Giles with all the mythical attributes
of a storybook hero.

It made her squirm to think about it now, but
Alicia could see just how embarrassing it must have
been for Giles to have a young sixteen-year-old girl
dogging his footsteps, and hanging on his every word
as if it were holy writ. Not that he had shown any
sign of it, of course. In fact, it was he who had

suggested that she and her chestnut pony, Rufus,
should join him in his early morning rides about the
estate. She, of course, had been in seventh heaven,
and had deliberately ignored and flouted Jed's
warnings to stay well away from the young Squire.
'You know nowt about owt!' he had shouted. 'You
mark my words! Your *precious* Mr Ratcliffe is only
after one thing—and then he'll toss you right back
on't dung heap where you belong. Just see if he
don't!'

The old sheepdog gave a yelp, sharply jerking
Alicia back to the present. 'Oh, I'm sorry, Rex,' she
murmured contritely, putting her arms about him as
she realised that she had been so absorbed by the
past that her tense fingers must have been stroking
him too roughly.

'God knows, I always disliked your master,' she
added, getting up to fill her hot-water bottle. 'But I
should have listened to him, shouldn't I? There's no
doubt that for the first and probably the only time in
his life, Jed was actually trying to do me a favour.'
She gave a grim laugh. 'He was absolutely right about
Giles Ratcliffe, wasn't he?'

CHAPTER THREE

ALICIA swore under her breath as she fought with the gear lever of Jed's rickety old Land Rover. It was many years since she had driven a four-wheel-drive vehicle, and from the sound of the coughs and wheezes coming from the engine, it would be a nine days' wonder if she and this rusty old heap ever arrived in Bridgnorth. She had warned the solicitor that she might be late, but she had been thinking more of the weather than the reliability of her transport—although the condition of the road was nothing to write home about, either. A snow plough had obviously been along earlier in the day, but there was still a hard base of treacherous black ice under the light sprinkling of snow, on which it was only too easy to skid out of control.

Polly had telephoned late last night to confirm her safe arrival in London, her call giving Alicia the opportunity to add some more essential items to the list. 'I think that's the lot . . .' she had said, scanning the piece of paper in her hand. 'Oh, yes, there doesn't seem to be any first-aid equipment up here, so can you bring all the bandages, plasters and ointment you can find? I know we probably won't need them,' she added, 'but it's just as well to be prepared for any emergency.'

Since her stepdaughter had never been known to be an early riser, Alicia hadn't expected her to arrive back at the farm until lunchtime at the earliest. Busily engaged after breakfast in feeding the calves, she was surprised to hear what seemed to be the roar of a super-charged engine. Putting down the bale of hay which she had been carrying, she went over to open the barn door, only to stand rooted to the ground as she stared at the approaching vehicle in stunned amazement.

'Hi, Ally—I bet you never expected to see me so soon!' Polly called out as she brought the long, low car to a halt.

'No—no, I didn't,' Alicia muttered. 'But what on earth are you doing with that—that . . .'

'Isn't it great? I just knew you'd love it.'

' "Love" isn't exactly the word I was thinking of!' Alicia didn't bother to even try to repress a shudder as she gazed at the car, which had been sprayed a particularly vivid, bilious shade of lime green. The colour was not enhanced by someone's happy thought of also adding some large white, painted daisies with acid-yellow centres, which twined their way all over the bright green car.

'Honestly, I've never driven so fast in all my life—I must have been doing at least a hundred and twenty down the motorway!' Polly enthused, as she left the car and came over to stand beside Alicia. 'And it's so comfortable, besides being able to carry masses of luggage.'

'But—but where's the Mini? And how—or where— did you find this monstrosity?'

'*Monstrosity . . .?* Don't be daft. This is a Ferrari, for heaven's sake!'

'Well, I suppose there's nothing wrong that a good pair of dark glasses and a quick re-spray wouldn't put right!' Alicia agreed, now that she could see the lean thoroughbred lines of the car beneath the extraordinary paintwork. 'However, I'm still waiting to hear what's happened to the Mini. You didn't crash it, I hope?'

'Honestly! No, of course I didn't. This lovely thing belongs to Rupert L'Aisie. He dropped in to see me last night, and when I was grumbling about how much I had to bring up here, and how I didn't see how it could all fit into the Mini—well, to cut a long story short, he said he'd lend me this car. He got done for drunken driving again last week—the stupid clot!—and has had his licence taken away. He told me I can keep it for as long as I like, which I must say is jolly nice of him.' She turned to look at Alicia's pale face. 'It doesn't seem as if you had much sleep last night. I *knew* I shouldn't have left you on your own. Was the old house very spooky?'

'No, of course not. I slept like a log,' Alicia said firmly, if untruthfully. In fact, it hadn't been the house, or even the thought of Jed's ghost, which had kept her awake until the early hours of this morning. Her restless state had been solely due to the memories of her unhappy love affair with Giles— a part of her 'murky past' which she definitely had no intention of discussing with Polly, either now or in the future.

'Well,' she continued briskly, 'Rupert clearly has more money than sense. I always thought that he was quite the stupidest of your boy-friends—and if I'd ever seen his car, I'd have known it for a fact! Whatever possessed him to paint it those ghastly colours?'

'I think the daisies are rather fun, but I can see that they're probably an acquired taste,' Polly grinned. 'It's just a joke on his name: L'Aisie—lazy daisy. Get it?'

Alicia groaned at the dreadful pun. 'Well, you'd better go in and let Elsie make you a hot cup of coffee while I finish feeding the calves. Then we'll unpack the car, before you hide that hideous thing permanently away in one of the barns.'

'Don't you want to drive it? We've got to have some form of transport, after all.'

'You must be kidding! Jed's old Land Rover will do very well for the time being. Believe me, I wouldn't be seen dead at the wheel of that ghastly eyesore,' Alicia had laughed. But now, as she inched her way up the steep hill of the old town, praying

that the ancient vehicle wouldn't stall, she did wonder
if maybe she wouldn't have been better off with the
Ferrari, however bizarre its appearance. She could
only hope and pray that the car park hadn't been
moved during the last eight years, because not only
had she yet to find the Land Rover's reverse gear,
but she also very much doubted whether its handbrake
was in working order.

Fifteen minutes later, and feeling years older by
the time she had managed to find somewhere to
park, she was ushered into Mr Pemberton's office.

She barely remembered the white-haired gentleman
who had been her parents' solicitor, but he rose and
greeted her with a twinkling smile, saying that he'd
have known her anywhere. 'You look just like your
dear mother. Ah, what a lovely girl she was! We
were all madly in love with her, you know. It quite
broke my heart when she married your father.'

Alicia smiled, both at his kind words, and at the
recollection that Mr Pemberton had always been
a very contented bachelor, carefully evading all
matrimonial traps and happily living on his own,
looked after by a devoted housekeeper.

'I was sorry to hear of your stepfather's demise in
the prime of life.' He shook his head sorrowfully.
'What times we live in—*O tempora, O mores!*
However, we must now turn to business,' he added
briskly. 'Mr Jed Black left a very simple will, of
which both you and I are the sole executors. Its
contents are very simple. He has, in essence, left
everything to you.'

'*To me* . . .?' Alicia looked at him in astonishment.
'Are you quite sure?'

'My dear young lady . . .'

'Oh, please—I didn't mean to be rude. It's just that
it's so unexpected.' She shrugged and frowned in
bewilderment.

Mr Pemberton gave a discreet cough. 'I can quite
understand your surprise in the light of your . . .

er . . . past association with your stepfather with whom, I understand, you did not always see eye to eye. However, I can assure you that he was quite certain of his intentions. I myself drew up his will some three years ago, and I feel quite confident that it properly expresses his wishes.'

There was a long silence as Alicia stared blindly at the elderly solicitor. 'I don't suppose it's any secret that Jed and I actively disliked each other,' she said at last. 'My first reaction was to assume that he was either drunk or out of his mind at the time he made his will. But if you say . . .'

'There is no doubt in my mind that Mr Black was perfectly sane,' Mr Pemberton assured her firmly. 'And despite whatever disagreements there might have been between you and your stepfather in the past, the fact remains that you are, *ipso facto*, the chief and only beneficiary of Mr Jed Black.' He cleared his throat and studied the papers in front of him. 'As you know, Winterfloods Farm, comprising the land, buildings and farmhouse, are at present held on a leased tenancy from Eastdale Hall Estate. Mr Jed Black, by virtue of the fact that he had been married to your mother, was awarded the tenancy when she died. It's very unfortunate that your father left no direct male heir. The lease, therefore, will now be terminated and the tenancy will undoubtedly revert to Mr Giles Ratcliffe, the owner of Eastdale Hall. However, the animals and machinery on the farm are yours, to dispose of as you see fit. It is usual, in such circumstances, to have a farm sale on the premises, but you can sell those items privately if you wish.'

Alicia frowned slightly. 'I understand the basic theory of the situation, but how does it all work out in practice? I mean, is the farm mine until I hand it over? And what about the house, which my family have lived in for such a long time?'

'You are in technical possession of the farm until it

is handed back to Mr Ratcliffe, and when I say "the farm", I'm afraid that it includes the farmhouse as well.' Mr Pemberton sighed. 'It is a great pity that your father didn't have a son to follow him. If he had, then under the Tenancy Act he would automatically inherit the tenancy of the farm—and his son after him—and there would be no problem.'

'Really, Mr Pemberton,' she remarked drily. 'That sounds remarkably like sex discrimination!'

'Not at all, Lady Preston, not at all!' He looked quite flustered for a moment. 'There would be nothing to prevent you yourself from claiming the tenancy if you so wished. You would, of course, have to prove that you were capable of farming the land, and satisfy other various criteria, but . . .'

'It's all right, I wasn't being entirely serious.' She smiled at the elderly man. 'When do I have to give the farm back to Mr Ratcliffe?'

'Most farms change hands on either Lady Day, which is March the twenty-fifth, or at Michaelmas in the autumn. Since we are now in the first week of March, I assume that Mr Ratcliffe would not wish to act with undue haste, and will undoubtedly decide to take back the land at Michaelmas. However, if you would like me to write to his agents and confirm that date, I will of course do so.'

Alicia, who had no wish to have *any* correspondence with Giles, either at first or second hand, quickly shook her head. 'No, I'd rather the matter was left alone for the time being. Thank you for all you've done,' she added, rising to her feet and preparing to leave.

'Oh, there is just one more thing I forgot to mention,' the solicitor said as he shook her hand. 'Mr Jed Black also left you the contents of his deposit account, which, you may be surprised to hear, amounts to well over fifty thousand pounds. As soon as we have probate of his estate, I'll send you a cheque for the full amount.'

Alicia's head was still spinning with confusion as she carefully drove the old Land Rover back to the farm along the heavily snow-packed road, praying that she wouldn't be stopped by a police car, since from the way the wheels were sliding over the icy surface, she very much suspected that all the tyres were practically bald.

Fifty thousand pounds! If the old skinflint had that amount of money tucked away, why on earth didn't he spend some of it on a decent tractor—or a new Land Rover, come to that? And what had Jed gained by squirrelling away all the farm profits, instead of spending some of the money on keeping the farmhouse and machinery in good condition? Surely there was a phrase about such miserliness in the Bible? Alicia smiled as she recalled the hell, fire and brimstone sermons of the Reverend Philip Ellis. The Rector of Eastdale had been well known for the down-to-earth, pointed remarks with which he would address some of the erring members of his congregation. That wicked old gossip, Mrs Jenkins, had always blithely ignored his oft-repeated quotation: 'Keep thy tongue from evil and speak no guile'; although Alicia could still remember the tremendous sensation one Sunday, when the schoolmaster's prim and proper wife had given a loud cry and fainted dead away during a sermon based on the text: 'A woman taken in adultery.' Alicia frowned as she hunted through her mind for one of Mr Ellis' favourite sayings about the hoarding of riches. How did it go . . .? Something about: 'Lay not up for yourselves treasures upon earth, where moth and rust doth currupt . . . but lay up for yourselves treasures in Heaven' . . .? Not that Jed's money was exactly a 'treasure', of course, but the moral truth behind the Rector's quotation was plainly evident. It very much looked as if Jed had killed himself as a direct result of his own tight-fisted miserliness.

Alicia gave a heavy sigh and tried to concentrate

on arriving back at the farm in one piece. The snow
was falling heavily once again, and she could hardly
see where she was going. The rubber blades of the
windscreen wipers were worn through and practically
useless, and although she was nearly home, the sky
seemed to be getting darker every minute. After
seeing Mr Pemberton, she had rushed around the
shops in Bridgnorth, buying as many of the essential
items on her shopping list as she could find. Several
of the shopkeepers had mentioned that a blizzard was
forecast, but she hadn't been able to spare the time
to lay in more than a few basic stores. Although Elsie
had always despised tinned and convenience foods,
they might well be glad of them if the weather turned
nasty. She could well remember one hard winter
when they had been completely snowed in for weeks.
The snowdrifts had been well over twelve feet high,
with forage for the starving animals having to be
dropped on the fields by helicopter. Alicia had only
been about ten years old at the time, and had found
it all very exciting, although she could recall just how
worried her father and mother had been.

Her thoughts were suddenly interrupted as she
noticed clouds of steam issuing from the bonnet of
the Land Rover.

'*Damn!* That's all I need!' she muttered, trying to
brake gently on the icy surface as she steered the
vehicle towards the side of the road. Praying that the
radiator hadn't cracked, she opened the door and got
out to lift the bonnet, only to discover that it was the
fan belt which had worn through.

It was only another mile back to the village, but
she hadn't a hope of making it, not unless she could
either find a spare fan belt, or improvise some form
of substitute. Moving gingerly in her high-heeled
court shoes over the slippery ice, she made her way
around to the back of the vehicle. 'Positive thought is
everything!' she said aloud in an attempt to keep up
her spirits, but the sound of her voice echoing in the

eerie silence of the deserted country road did little to help her feel more optimistic.

It took her some time to sort through the boxes of farm tools, cardboard cartons and heavy coils of rope. The ropes had looked quite promising at first, but she soon discovered that there was nothing with which to cut the short length she needed. Half an hour later, after realising that she had been hunting in vain, Alicia was not only in a furious temper, but grimly determined not to be beaten. There had to be *something* she could do, she told herself desperately, and then suddenly wondered if it wasn't possible to use one of her stockings as a substitute for the broken fan belt. She quickly climbed inside the back of the Land Rover, trying not to think about the state of her smart Saint Laurent suit, which Polly had brought up from London this morning. Although an entirely suitable garment for seeing Mr Pemberton, it was hardly designed for clambering about in a filthy dirty farm vehicle. Sitting perched on an empty oil drum, she was just removing the thin silk from her leg when she heard the sound of a car drawing up. Smiling with relief at the thought of rescue, she groaned under her breath as she looked back over her shoulder to see Giles' dark head peering in through the open window by the driver's seat.

'Oh dear,' he drawled. 'Whatever possessed you to take this piece of scrap iron out on to the road—and especially in this sort of weather?'

'I had to go into Bridgnorth,' Alicia muttered, inwardly cursing her rotten luck. It *would* have to be Giles who'd turned up to rescue her, wouldn't it?'

'Well, well,' he grinned, coming around to open the door at the rear of the vehicle. 'I've seen some sights in my time, but I don't think that I can ever remember seeing anyone do a strip-tease in a Land Rover before!'

'Oh, very funny!' she scowled. Not only was it freezing cold, especially now that the rear door was

open, but she was fed up to the back teeth with the
dreadful old vehicle. The very last thing she needed
was for Giles to be standing there, making stupid
jokes and laughing himself silly at her expense. In
fact, she only wished that he was within reach, so
that she could have the considerable pleasure and
satisfaction of slapping that smarmy grin off his
handsome face.

'Why in the hell don't you just go away and leave
me alone?' she ground out angrily.

'What? Desert a damsel in distress? How could you
possibly believe that I'm the sort of man to do that?'
he mocked, his grin widening as he noticed that she
was trying to hide her bare leg. 'I'm sure there's a
perfectly rational explanation, but I can't help
wondering why you've taken off one of your stockings.
Not that I'm complaining, of course—in fact, I'm
quite willing to help you remove the other!'

Gritting her teeth and clamping her lips tightly
shut, Alicia managed to hang on to her temper. He
was just trying to get a rise out of her, so why should
she give him the satisfaction of responding to his
deliberately offensive remarks.

'If you must know,' she said, when she felt she
could trust her voice, 'the fan belt has broken. I
couldn't find a spare, or anything else for that matter,
and then it occurred to me that one of my stockings
might do as a substitute.'

'That's not a bad idea, and it might just work,'
Giles said thoughtfully. 'What a clever, resourceful
girl you are! However, may I suggest that a quicker,
easier and warmer alternative would be for me to
give you a lift back to the farm. You can then get
Johnny Knight at the garage to collect this rusty
heap—although I doubt if even he'll be able to do
anything with it.'

His remarks so accurately reflected her own opinion
of the ancient Land Rover that Alicia couldn't quarrel
with what he said. But however much she might

curse her bad luck at being found by Giles, there was no point in being a martyr by refusing his help—especially as she had to get back fairly soon to feed the animals.

'Oh, all right. It doesn't look as if I've any alternative,' she grumbled. 'However, I'm not putting my stocking on again with you standing there. Go and sit in your car, and I'll join you in a minute.'

'I have seen your bare legs before, Alicia,' he drawled, his grey eyes gleaming with amusement at her predicament. 'Even though "Lady Preston" might not want to be reminded of that fact.'

'You're quite right—she doesn't!' she snapped angrily. 'Now buzz off!'

'Tsk, tsk. We mustn't lose our temper!' he taunted, before closing the door and walking back to his own vehicle.

Alicia took a deep breath, letting it out on a long sigh. This was hardly the scenario she had envisaged when she had reluctantly allowed Elsie to persuade her to return to Eastdale for Jed's funeral. She had wondered about the possibility of seeing Giles, but had considered it a remote one, since she had only been intending to pay a fleeting visit. And now . . .? Not only was she trapped at the farm for the foreseeable future, but the damned man kept turning up like a bad penny—first at the funeral, and now here, miles from anywhere.

It really did seem as if fate was throwing rotten tomatoes in her direction, Alicia thought gloomily, lapsing for a moment into a morass of self-pity. Nothing was turning out as she had imagined, and she had the horrible feeling of being stuck on an escalator that was travelling in quite the wrong direction, and from which she couldn't dismount however hard she tried to do so.

Come on! You've got to pull yourself together, she told herself firmly, bending down to pull up her stocking. It was no good moaning on about the fickle finger of fate, when in a few moments she was going to have to join Giles. If she wanted to avoid any discussion of their past relationship, or his marriage to Camilla, she'd better try and think of some bright, innocuous topic of conversation that would keep them both occupied during the five-mile drive back to the farm.

Collecting her handbag and parcels from the front seat, Alicia stepped down and walked over to where Giles' Range Rover was waiting.

'You took your time,' he said, leaning across to open the door.

'A woman's prerogative, surely?' she answered lightly, settling into her seat and slamming the door.

Giles laughed. 'You're so right! I've never yet known a woman to be on time for anything.'

'And you've known so many, haven't you?' she retorted quickly.

There was a long pause as her caustic words echoed around the enclosed space. A moment later he had grasped her chin with a firm hand, turning her face towards him, and fixing her with an unwavering stare from his hard grey eyes, 'If you want a lift, I suggest that you remember your manners,' he informed her bluntly. 'You can either decide to keep that sweet mouth of yours firmly shut—or get out and start walking. Which is it to be?'

Alicia's cheeks flushed, her eyes sliding nervously away from his hard, steely gaze. He was right. There had been no need for her to make such an unnecessary, uncalled-for remark.

'Well . . .?'

'I—I'm sorry, Giles. I . . .' she swallowed convulsively, all her senses acutely aware of the dynamic, masculine aura of the man sitting so near to her. She could almost feel the energy and tension emanating from his broad-shouldered body, and the

aromatic scent of his aftershave filled her nostrils.
She gave a tense, nervous shiver as his head came
closer, so close that his breath fanned her cheek,
staring mesmerised up at the mouth over her own,
a sick, trembling excitement running like liquid fire
through her veins. And then, almost shockingly,
the hard fingers cupping her jaw pushed her head
abruptly away.

'You'd better do up your seat belt,' he said flatly,
waiting until she had complied before he set the car
in motion.

Alicia averted her head, staring blindly out of the
window as she tried to pull herself together. What
on earth was wrong with her, for heaven's sake?
She'd accepted a lift from Giles with the avowed
intention of being friendly and polite, and yet within
the space of a few seconds, she'd been quite
unnecessarily rude and aggressive. And why she
should now have such a sick, aching void deep in
her stomach she had no idea. She was just tired,
that was all. Of course he hadn't been going to kiss
her just now! Ever since she had left London she
had been feeling almost unbearably fraught and
tense, so it was no wonder that her imagination
seemed to be getting out of control . . . She really
must try to calm down and stop over-reacting, she
thought, glancing sideways through her lashes at
Giles' profile. He was concentrating on the road,
his lips set in a hard line, his hands tightly gripping
the wheel. She really hadn't any choice—she was
going to have to apologise, if only to attempt to
dispel the tense atmosphere inside the vehicle.

'I'm sorry if I was rude just now,' she said
quietly. 'I—well, I expect it was because I was so
fed up with that dreadful old Land Rover, although
I do realise that I shouldn't have taken my bad
temper out on you.'

He sighed, his tall body relaxing as he leaned
back in his seat. 'Forget it—it was as much my fault

as yours. I shouldn't have teased you when you were obviously cold and tired.' He turned his head to give her a brief, wry smile. 'We do seem to have got off on the wrong foot with each other since your return to the village, don't we?'

'Yes. I . . .' Alicia hesitated, giving an unhappy shrug of her shoulders as she turned to gaze out of the window. How could she possibly try to explain her complicated feelings for the man sitting beside her? The instinctive, gut reaction when in his presence which led her to become rude and aggressive, the overwhelming need to hurt and wound him as much as possible. She, who had always prided herself on her cool, calm acceptance of life, was now feeling totally bewildered and confused by her own behaviour, over which she seemed to have so little control.

'Eastdale is a small village, and we'll undoubtedly be seeing a certain amount of each other,' he said, swinging the car off the main road and driving down the lane towards the farm. 'I don't want to quarrel with you, Alicia. Might it not be a good idea to forget what we've said to each other over the past two days—and maybe try to begin again, hmm?' he added as he brought the vehicle to a halt in the farmyard.

Alicia bent down, struggling to undo her seat belt. 'I agree that it's . . . Whoever does that car belong to?' she exclaimed as she looked up to see a yellow estate car parked outside the farm house.

'It looks remarkably like Bob Cooper's Volvo.' Giles opened his door and went over to peer through the rear window of the strange car. 'Yes, I thought so. Bob is our local vet,' he explained, coming back to help her alight.

'The vet? Oh, lord! I hope nothing disastrous has happened,' she said, quickly gathering up her parcels and hurrying across the yard towards the house.

'Ah—my dear mama, at last! What took you so

long? I expected you back ages ago—in fact, I was getting quite worried about you,' Polly said as Alicia rushed into the kitchen.

'That's nothing to how I felt when Giles said the vet was here! Is there a problem with one of the animals?' Alicia asked the strange young man, who put down his cup of tea and rose from the table.

'There's no need to worry,' he assured her. 'It was just a simple case of two ewes dropping their lambs in the paddock, and . . .'

'It's all my stupid fault,' Polly cut in quickly. 'I mean, I've never seen an animal give birth before, and I completely lost my cool, I'm afraid. Not knowing what to do, I grabbed the phone directory and found Bob's name heading the list of vets.' She smiled up at the young man. 'It was terribly kind of him to come straight out here, especially since it appears to have been a complete waste of time.'

'Are the sheep all right?' Alicia asked anxiously.

The vet gave her a reassuring smile. 'They're fine, and so are their lambs. You've got nothing to worry about, although if this weather continues I'd advise you to get the rest of the animals under some sort of cover.'

'An excellent suggestion, and the sooner the better.' Alicia jumped as Giles spoke from behind her. 'I've just had a look at those ewes in the paddock, and I'd say that some of them are ready to have their lambs any day now,' he added, walking over to warm his hands on the stove. 'Is there any more tea in that pot?' he asked Polly. 'Because, if so, I think your stepmother could do with some hot liquid inside her. I'll just go and phone Knight's garage. With any luck they'll be able to collect the Land Rover before it gets too dark,' he added, striding across the kitchen towards the farm office.

Polly, who had raised a quizzical eyebrow at Giles' appearance, and the fact that he seemed to know his way around the farmhouse, turned quickly

to Alicia. 'Did you have an accident? I *knew* you
should have taken the Ferrari and left that rusty old
heap strictly alone. You aren't hurt, are you . . .?'

'Relax!' Alicia smiled. 'The "rusty old heap" did
break down, but as you can see, I'm quite safe and
sound. Luckily, before I got too cold, I was rescued
by Mr Ratcliffe.' She turned as Giles re-entered the
room. 'By the way, I don't think you've met each
other. This is my stepdaughter, Polly Preston.'

'Hi. We have met, actually,' said Polly, grinning
at his blank expression as she poured two more
cups of tea. 'Yesterday—outside the churchyard.
You seemed in a bit of a hurry, and not—er—not
exactly in the best of moods at the time!'

'Very possible,' Giles said drily. 'The garage are
going to pick the Land Rover up,' he told Alicia
before nodding at the vet. 'Hello, Bob. Any
problems?'

'No, sir. Everything here seems to be well under
control. Miss Preston's call was paged through to
me on the radio telephone in my car while I was
seeing to one of your cows at Hall Farm. Your
foreman was a bit upset when I had to confirm that
the cow had brucellosis.'

'Oh, hell! That means notifying the Ministry and
destroying the animal, I suppose?'

'I'm afraid so.'

'What about the rest of the herd?' Giles asked,
going over to sit down at the table beside the vet.

'I feel such an idiot,' muttered Polly as she came
over to where Alicia was standing, and handing her
a cup of tea. 'Those two ewes didn't need any help
at all, and in fact it was all over by the time that
chap turned up.'

'If I didn't know anything about sheep, I'd
probably have done exactly the same thing,' Alicia
reassured her. 'Besides, I'm bound to need the
vet's assistance sooner or later, so it's just as well
that we now know who to ring in an emergency,'

she said, glancing over at the two men who were
deep in discussion. 'He seems a very nice man.'

'Yes, he is—and very helpful. When I told him
how interested I was in getting to know more about
farming, he said he'd take me out with him on his
rounds.'

'I don't think we're going to be staying here long
enough for that,' she cautioned the younger girl.

Polly shrugged. 'That's not what Elsie says. She
reckons that we'll have to stay here at the farm for
at least a month—probably longer.'

'Elsie's talking through her hat,' Alicia said firmly.
'Where is she, by the way?'

'To use her own words, she "came all over
queer", and so I took her home. I must say that she
didn't look at all well.' Polly frowned in concern.
'Do you think she can have caught the 'flu from her
husband?'

'It sounds as though she might have. I'll go along
to her cottage and see her later. But first of all, I
have to get those sheep out of the paddock and into
the large barn before it gets too dark.' Alicia put
down her empty cup and walked over to the door.
'Thank you for rescuing me, Giles,' she said,
avoiding his eyes as she turned to smile at the
young vet. 'Both Polly and I are very grateful for
your help, Mr Cooper. And now, if you'll excuse
me, I must go and get into some working clothes.'

Taking some of the parcels upstairs, Alicia quickly
took off the smart London suit she had worn to see
Mr Pemberton, and put on one of the new pairs of
jeans that she had brought in Bridgnorth. Rum-
maging through the pile of clothes that Polly had
brought up from London, and which she hadn't had
time to put away in her drawers, she found a red
woollen shirt and a heavy dark blue Guernsey
sweater.

Standing in front of a mirror as she piled her
long, ash-blonde hair up on top of her head, she

tried to ignore the extraordinary sensation of *déjà vu* engendered by the sight of her slim, jean-clad figure. It was almost frightening to see how little she had changed. Stripped of her sophisticated clothes, and with her face bare of make-up, she looked almost exactly the same girl who had stood here over eight years ago. So young and naïve, so hopefully and ecstatically in love with Giles . . .

'You've got to stop thinking about the past—it's dead and gone!' she whispered savagely at her reflection, her words accompanied by the distant sound of voices and the noise of a car being driven away. It looked as if Giles had gone back to the Hall, which was just as well since there was no doubt that the less she had to do with him, the better. It was kind of him to have rescued her from the old Land Rover, and she was grateful not to be still stuck out on the road, quietly freezing to death. But that was it. As far as she was concerned, Giles Ratcliffe was bad news, and she had every intention of avoiding any further contact with him as though he had the plague!

Running downstairs, she walked quickly along the corridor towards the kitchen. 'If you'll just give me a hand with the sheep, Polly, I'll go and . . . and . . .' Her voice trailed away, her eyes widening with confusion as she saw that the room was empty—save for the figure of Giles, who was lying back in a chair with his feet up on the stove.

'You took your time getting changed,' he murmured, turning his head to view her still, rigid figure.

'Where's Polly?' she demanded.

'She's gone off with young Bob Cooper. A farmer nearby has some sows due to farrow, and I think she's rather keen to get in on the act! I must say, it's a long time since I met such a funny and amusing girl!' he laughed, swinging his feet down and slowly rising from the chair. 'There's no need to look so shocked,' he added as she stood staring blankly at his tall figure. 'Although he seemed very taken by Polly, I can assure you that Bob is a very respectable young man. She'll be quite safe with him.'

'Yes . . . no . . . I mean, yes—I know she will . . .' Alicia muttered. What on earth was he talking about? Of course she had no need to worry about Polly—that strong-minded girl was more than capable of dealing with the Bob Coopers of this world! But Giles was quite another kettle of fish, she thought, eyeing him apprehensively.

'Come on, Alicia. There's no point in you standing there in a daydream,' he drawled mockingly. 'We've got work to do.'

I know what work *I've* got to do—which consists of getting the sheep out of the paddock and into the barn,' she replied coolly. 'However, I fail to see how it has anything to do with you. I don't want to appear rude, but isn't it time you went home?'

Giles gave a heavy sigh. 'Why do you think I've been waiting here in the kitchen? You can't possibly do the job on your own.'

'Oh, yes, I can,' she snapped.

'No, you damn well can't!' he retorted curtly. 'So stop being so ridiculously pig-headed, and let's get on with the job. You might not want my help,' he added as she continued to glare mutinously at him. 'But you ought to be thinking of those poor ewes out there, and not your own finer feelings.'

'Oh—*all right!*' she grumbled, stalking past him into the scullery.

'And don't forget to wrap up warmly; it's freezing out there, and you don't want to catch pneumonia.'

'I'm quite capable of looking after myself, thank you! You're the one who ought to be worried. Those smart shoes of yours are going to be worse than useless,' Alicia informed him bluntly as she pulled on her Wellingtons, longing to give way to an almost irresistable urge to clout him about the head with one of the heavy rubber boots.

'I'm sorry to disappoint you, but I do have a pair of boots in the Range Rover!' Giles gave a short bark of sardonic laughter. 'Come on, Alicia. Stop sulking, and let's get on with the job, hmm?'

CHAPTER FOUR

MUCH later that night, as Alicia sat wearily in the kitchen drinking a hot cup of cocoa, she couldn't remember the last time she had felt quite so tired and exhausted.

Despite Giles' help—and she was quite willing to admit freely that she could never have managed without his assistance—it had taken some considerable time before they got all the sheep into the barn. The swiftly falling darkness had hindered the operation, it being difficult to make sure that some of the ewes weren't hiding beyond the beam of their torches. At one point she had thought of trying to use Rex, but had been forced to discard that idea, because she didn't know the commands and whistles used by Jed to control and direct his sheepdog. So it had been a matter of trial and error as they attempted to drive the flock of sheep to where—as it quickly transpired—they clearly had no intention of going.

'I've never seen such damned stupid animals in all my life!' Alicia had shouted in exasperation, and her words had been mild to those uttered by Giles, when he slipped on a piece of ice and fell into a small dung heap in the farmyard. That had made her laugh so much that he had retaliated by throwing a snowball at her. Whereupon a free-for-all battle had commenced, which was only terminated when Alicia dashed for cover through the large open entrance of the barn. Minutes later they were both leaning up against the thick stone walls, helpless with laughter.

'We must be out of out minds!' Alicia gasped,

when she managed to catch her breath. 'Anyone would think we were a couple of kids . . .!'

'Who cares? I haven't had so much fun for years!' he panted, putting an arm about her shoulders and drawing her close to his tall body.

'Pooh! You stink to high heaven!' she exclaimed, wrinkling her nose at the smell of dung which still clung to his clothes.

He grinned. 'I thought as how you was a country girl, wot was used to that there aroma, my dearie-o!' he drawled in a broad accent, the smile slowly dying on his lips as he stared down into her blue eyes. And then, almost before she knew what was happening, he had quickly stripped off his heavy jacket, tossing it aside as he roughly clasped her in his arms.

Trying to think rationally about the incident later that night, Alicia completely failed to understand her own lack of resistance to what happened next. Of course she had been feeling very tired. The strenuous physical exertion required to drive the sheep into the barn had been exhausting, and the snowball fight had possible drained most of her remaining energy. But that was hardly a valid excuse for weakly allowing him to undo her coat, nor for the dangerous languor with which she savoured the warmth of the body pressed so closely to her own.

'Alicia!' he groaned, burying his face in her hair. She could feel his heavy, ragged breath fanning her ear and the rapid thud of his heart beat. 'Oh, my God . . .!' he grated harshly, lifting his head to stare down at her, his flint-grey eyes glittering in the dim light. 'Have you any idea of what having you in my arms does to me?'

Like a rabbit trapped by the headlights of a car, Alicia could only gaze blindly up at him, helpless to prevent her treacherous body from instinctively responding to his close proximity. An age seemed to pass as his arms slowly tightened about her trembling form, his features growing hard and taut with tension.

And then, with almost shocking suddenness, his mouth claimed hers, possessing her lips with a kiss of such burning intensity that desire seemed to explode like a firework deep inside her.

Locked in his arms, she became lost to all sense of time and place. She was only aware of a feverish, long-denied hunger, a compulsive need to respond to the fierce invasive heat of his tongue, the scorching excitement provoked by the feel of his hands caressing her body.

It wasn't until a heavy weight thudded against the back of her knees, almost sweeping her feet from beneath her, that she began to regain her senses. Struggling to release herself from Giles' embrace, she received another hard nudge, and realised that it was only the strength of his arms which was enabling her to stand upright. Twisting her head to look back over her shoulder, it took her glazed eyes some seconds to realise that they were completely surrounded by a small group of heavily pregnant sheep, the majority of the flock moving swiftly out through the open door of the barn, clearly determined to return to their pasture.

'Alicia!' Giles muttered urgently, raising a hand to grasp her chin and forcing her head back to face him. 'I've got to tell you . . .'

'*Never mind that!*' she yelled, waving her arms like a windmill as she struggled to retain her balance. 'The damn sheep are trying to get back to the paddock. Quick! We'll have to try and cut them off. *Ah . . .!*'

As he glanced around the large stone barn, Giles had relaxed his firm grip of her body, and Alicia was unable to prevent herself from toppling backwards over a large woolly sheep, to fall with a thump on the dusty barn floor. Cursing violently under her breath, she staggered to her feet, throwing Giles' jacket over to him before running through the open door and back across the yard as fast as her boots would carry her.

It was another hour before all the ewes were safely herded into the barn, both Alicia and Giles being far too busy to say anything, other than call directions or instructions to one another as they rounded up the stray animals. It was only when he was helping her to close the heavy wooden doors, and Alicia was at last able to think of matters other than sheep, that she began to realise that she had placed herself in a very awkward predicament. That rampantly sexual encounter between them earlier in the barn seemed totally unreal, somehow. What on earth had come over her? She was entirely at a loss, completely unable to comprehend her own quite extraordinary behaviour. It was no good trying to pretend that, because she had been surprised and taken unawares, she had merely been a passive victim of his unbridled lust. As much as she loathed having to face the fact, the shocking truth was only too self-evident: there had been nothing passive about her response to his embrace, and if anyone was guilty of 'unbridled lust,' that person was her! So, what on earth was she going to say or do now . . .?

Grateful for the darkness which hid her fiercely burning cheeks, she pushed the heavy iron bar down over the closed doors and hesitantly began moving back towards the farmhouse.

'Just a minute,' Giles said firmly, catching hold of her arm and turning her around to face him. 'You and I have some unfinished business . . .'

'No!' she interrupted quickly. 'I mean . . . well . . . I'm very grateful for your help. You were quite right . . . I'd never have got those sheep into the barn on my own . . . I'd quite forgotten how difficult they can be . . .' she gabbled, her last words drowned by the sound of a vehicle arriving in the yard. Temporarily dazzled by the headlights, she almost sagged with relief as Giles let go of her arm and she realised that Polly and the vet had returned in the nick of time.

The seventh cavalry to the rescue! Alicia thought, smiling at Polly who dashed over to where she and Giles were standing.

'I've had an absolutely super time! We simply *must* have some pigs! How did you get on with the sheep? It seems to have taken you a long time.'

'Yes, it did, unfortunately. However, I was just about to offer Giles a stiff drink, and I expect you'd like one too, Bob? So why don't we all go back into the kitchen and get warm?' Alicia asked, being careful to avoid looking at the stiff, rigid figure standing beside her.

'Thank you for the offer, but I have another appointment,' said Giles coldly, stalking off towards his Range Rover without another word.

'I'm afraid that I can't stay, either, Lady Preston.' Bob Cooper shook his head regretfully. 'If I don't get a move on, I'm going to be late for this evening's surgery.'

'Hmm . . . Yon Wicked Squire was in a bit of a hurry to leave, wasn't he?' Polly said as she waved goodbye to the young vet and walked back into the house with Alicia. 'By the way, I'm sorry I wasn't here to help you with the sheep. But when Bob offered to take me to look at some pigs, your Mr Ratcliffe seemed to think it was the best idea since sliced bread—and practically threw me out of the house!'

'He's not *my* Mr Ratcliffe!' Alicia snapped, before sinking down wearily into a kitchen chair.

'Okay, okay, keep your hair on!' Polly murmured, viewing her stepmother with concern. 'You seem dead beat. Why don't I pour you a stiff drink—you certainly look as if you could do with it.'

'That's about the best suggestion I've heard today.' Alicia gave her a tired, wry smile. 'And then I'm going to have a long hot bath, followed by an early supper and bed, because I'm absolutely pooped!'

'Never mind,' Polly said over her shoulder as she went to fetch a neat whisky. 'You can take things easy tomorrow.'

Alicia sighed. 'I wish I could,' she muttered. Unfortunately, she knew she couldn't just leave the sheep to mill around in the barn. 'We're going to have to set up wattle hurdles, so that we can pen the ewes into small groups. It makes it far easier to cope with them when they're having their lambs,' she explained as Polly placed a glass in her hand. 'So don't worry about not having been here to help me get them down from the paddock. You'll have ample opportunity tomorrow to find out just how stubborn, and irritating, those silly sheep can be!'

Polly had obviously thought that she'd been unnecessarily gloomy. But sitting here, now, in the quiet kitchen, warming her hands around her cup of cocoa and making a list of all the things she had to do tomorrow, Alicia knew that she hadn't exaggerated. And it wasn't just a case of the sheep. Before going up to have her bath, she had phoned Elsie. As she had feared, it seemed that the old housekeeper had caught the 'flu from her husband. 'But don't you worry none, I'll be right as a tick tomorrow,' Elsie had said in a thin, reedy voice.

'Oh, no, you won't! You're to go to bed and stay there,' Alicia had said firmly. 'And don't you dare come back to the farm until the doctor says you can.'

Expecting to have a battle royal with Elsie, she had been surprised and then worried when the older woman hadn't argued, meekly agreeing that maybe she could do with a few days' rest.

Making a note to remind herself to call at the housekeeper's cottage first thing in the morning, Alicia finished her hot drink and went over to the stove to fill her hot-water bottle. As well as running the farm, it was clear that she was also going to have

to do the cooking from now on, and that presented
quite a problem. There had always been plenty of
staff at the house in London, and in fact Mrs Simpson,
the chauffeur's wife, would have been deeply upset—
not to say mortally offended—if Alicia had ever tried
to usurp her iron rule in the kitchen. Not that she
had ever attempted to do so, since Mrs Simpson was
a superb cook, but now she found herself desperately
wishing that she'd paid more attention to the culinary
arts when her mother had been alive.

Trailing slowly upstairs to bed, Alicia knew that
she had been deliberately avoiding all thought of
Giles, and their passionate encounter out in the barn.
She had determinedly blocked all thought of the
episode from her mind, and she had no intention of
remembering it now, she told herself firmly as she got
into bed. In fact, she had every intention of trying to
forget that anything at all had happened, and if she
couldn't—then, like Scarlett O'Hara, she would think
about it tomorrow.

As matters turned out, Alicia was kept far too busy
the next morning to have the time to think about
anything other than pressing farm business. From the
moment she was shaken awake by Polly—who
announced that there was a lorry in the yard, and
where was the driver to unload the cattle food which
had been ordered by Jed some weeks ago?—it was all
systems go.

Added to the usual chores of feeding and mucking
out the cattle, she and Polly had also to do the same
for the flock of sheep in the barn. It wasn't until
eleven o'clock that they found the time for a quick
coffee break, and even then, Alicia had hardly
managed to have a sip of the hot liquid before she
heard the phone ringing in the office. Lifting the
receiver, she found that it was a call from Knight's
garage in the village. As instructed by Mr Ratcliffe,
they had retrieved the Land Rover last night; it now

had a new fan belt and was ready for collection at
any time.

'Can you give me lift into the village, Polly?' she
asked as she came back into the kitchen. 'It seems
the Land Rover had been mended, and I might as
well call at the local shop as well. Lord knows what
I'm going to cook us for lunch, but I thought if all
else fails, we might have some fresh bread and
cheese.' She frowned. 'Oh, heavens, I've completely
forgotten that I meant to go and see how Elsie is
getting on.'

'That's no problem. I can call on her when I've
dropped you off at the garage. Incidentally,' Polly
grinned, 'I can't wait to see what culinary masterpiece
you're intending to serve up for my delectation!'

'Watch it, Polly! I've got a feeling that I'm not
going to find the subject at all funny. And in fact,
just one more ribald comment from you, and you're
likely to find yourself doing the cooking instead of
me, okay?'

The younger girl looked at her with alarm. 'God
forbid! With that dire threat hanging over me, I can
promise total silence on the subject.'

Alicia kept her eyes firmly shut as the Ferrari
roared down the village street. God knows what the
local inhabitants would make of the extraordinary
vehicle, she thought, relieved when she could get out
and wave Polly on her way.

As always, the tumbledown garage appeared to be
deserted, it taking her some time and a great deal of
heavy thuds on the closed door to produce any
answer.

'Awl right, awl right! I ain't hard of hearing, nor I
ain't blind, neither!' called out a young man, ambling
slowly around the side of the dilapidated building.
'Well, well! he grinned, 'if it ain't little Alicia
Howard!'

'Hello, Johnny,' she said, smiling as she remembered
how, as young children, she and Johnny Knight used

to be partners in crime, scrumping apples and plums from the Rector's orchard.

'I did hear as how you was back for ol' Jed's funeral. Decided to stay on at the farm for a bit, have you?'

'Yes, I'm here for a few days. I believe you've got Jed's old Land Rover here for me. Can you fill it up with petrol and check the oil? I could do with some new blades for the windscreen wipers too, if you've got any.'

He led the way around the back to where the vehicle was parked, scowling as he gave the wheels a hard kick. 'Dang waste of time keeping this ol' thing on the road. You wants a slap bang-up motor—like Squire's new Porsche, fer instance.' He winked and gave her a sly grin. 'I knows where I can find one, real cheap.'

Alicia laughed. 'I bet you can. "Fell off a lorry", did it? Or haven't you nicked it yet?'

'Hang about! What do you takes me for?'

'A thorough-going rogue, of course!'

Johnny looked at her indignantly for a moment, and then gave a loud guffaw of laughter. 'For all you is now *Lady Preston*, I reckons that you ain't changed that much neither, my girl! I well remembers the time you and I let off them stink bombs in the village hall, and how we got tanned for climbing on the church roof, and . . .'

'Yes, well, that was a very long time ago,' Alicia said quickly. 'I know this vehicle is on its last legs, Johnny, but can you give it a quick check while I go over and get some things from the shop?'

He shrugged, wiping his hands on an oily rag and opening the bonnet. 'Yeah, I'll do what I can, but I reckons it's ready for the scrap heap.'

The tinkling bell on the door signalled her arrival as Alicia entered the village shop. The interior was deserted, and she took the opportunity to look around at the products placed higgledy-piggledy, in chaotic disorder on the various shelves. It was still exactly the same as when she had left eight years ago. Mrs Jenkins, who must undoubtedly have a mind like a computer, was the only person who knew exactly where everything was kept, changing the packets on the shelves every week in what was clearly a deliberate effort to confuse her customers. It had taken Alicia years to work out the strategy behind such a bewildering display of goods, eventually coming to the conclusion that Mrs Jenkins liked to keep her victims immobile—caught helplessly in a web—while she sucked them dry of information. Alicia was still smiling at the thought of Mrs Jenkins in the not inappropriate role of a black widow spider, when a woman emerged from somewhere at the back of the shop, and came up to the large wooden counter.

'My word, it's Miss Alicia, isn't it?'

'Hello, Mrs Jenkins,' she said, bracing herself for the forthcoming confrontation.

'Well, well—what a surprise!'

Who's she kidding? She undoubtedly knew I was coming back to Eastdale before I did! Alicia thought sourly, as she smiled non-committally at the older woman. Mrs Jenkins' clear, guileless blue eyes and her soft, warm expression gave no hint of the mind like a steel trap which lay carefully hidden beneath the fluffy grey curls. No one, looking at the dear, sweet old lady, could possibly believe what a wicked gossip she was—a fact that had led to the downfall of many in the village.

'I thought I'd lay in some extra provisions,' Alicia said, taking a notebook out of her handbag. 'I don't want to get caught if the weather turns bad.'

'Shocking amount of snow we're having. Are you going to be staying long?'

'Just a few days. Now, I'd like some bread, flour, sugar, butter, eggs and cheese,' she added firmly.

'Oh, dear, I haven't given you my condolences about poor Mr Black,' the older woman said as she

walked slowly over to a shelf. 'It was a terrible way
to go, wasn't it? Quite turned me up when I heard
about it, and a nasty upset for you, I expect . . .?'

'Yes.'

'Still, he was always a hard, difficult man, wasn't
he?' She shook her head sorrowfully as she gathered
up the packets of sugar. 'Few people will mourn his
passing, and that's a fact; I dare say he didn't have
many relatives to claim his money . . .?'

Alicia, determined not to give away any infromation,
just shrugged her shoulders and pretended to consult
her list.

'Not that you'll be in any want. I do hear tell that
you made a real good marriage, and that your late
husband left you very comfortably off—and so he
should, a lovely looking girl like you. It's *Lady*
Preston now, isn't it?' Mrs Jenkins gave a light,
tinkling laugh. 'Well, I always likes to see a girl get
on in the world. Although there was some as who'd
say you could have had Mr Ratcliffe, if you'd a
mind . . .?'

'Can you make that two pounds of cheese, please,'
Alicia said quickly.

'Right you are, m'dear. Yes, I always had a little
thought, tucked away at the back of my mind, that
you and the Squire was real fond of each other. And
there's no saying what would have happened, if you
hadn't gone off to London and left him all alone, the
poor man.'

'I didn't, I . . .' Alicia protested, before hurriedly
clamping her lips tightly together. Oh, *damn*! That
beastly old woman knew she was on the scent of
something—one quick glance at the sparkle in Mrs
Jenkins' guileless blue eyes confirmed her avid interest
in Alicia's past. Well, two could play at that game.

'I went to London because I had a job waiting for
me,' she lied airily. 'As for Mr Ratcliffe—I used to
see a lot of him when I was a child, particularly since
he was a good friend of my father's. But when my

mother married Jed, and I went off to boarding school, we more or less lost touch with him. He was years older than me, of course.' She gave a casual shrug. 'It's so long ago, that I can hardly remember the details, but wasn't he engaged to be married? I think I might have met his fiancée once or twice. She seemed a very nice girl.'

And make what you can of that! Alicia thought, smiling blandly at the older woman, who was clearly disappointed at not having gained any juicy snippets of information.

'It seems I must have been wrong about you and the Squire,' Mrs Jenkins conceded. 'And more's the pity, because that wife of his—well, m'dear, you'd never believe the goings on up at the Hall!'

'Really?' Alicia murmured in a bored voice. 'I think I'd better have some bacon,' she added, going over to look at a shelf of tinned fruit.

'Oh, yes, it was all fancy men in their fast cars— right from the day she married Mr Ratcliffe. That Camilla Harrison, I *knew* she was no good, right from the moment I saw the girl. Well, it stands to reason, don't it? There was her rich father, ready to give the girl anything she wanted—and what did she do?'

Mrs Jenkins leant confidentially across the counter, quite forgetting, in the excitement of relating the scandalous behaviour of the Squire's wife, that she had originally intended to interrogate Alicia.

'A "boutique"—that's what she called it,' the older woman continued. 'But she never had more'n one dress at a time in the window of that shop of hers in Shrewsbury. What sort of business was that, I'd like to know?'

'Undoubtedly an exclusive and expensive dress shop,' said Alicia drily.

'That's as may be, but I do know she gave her old father grey hairs, the way she carried on, and mighty glad he was when she married Mr Ratcliffe. But did that stop her? Oh, dear me, no—the flighty piece! The marriage only lasted one year, before the hussy ran away with that racehorse trainer what's always in the papers. And what's she doing now? Living with him, bold as brass—that's what! Terrible, I call it— really shocking. And poor Mr Ratcliffe left on his own, and ready to fall prey to that Mrs Todd.'

Alicia knew she'd regret it, but she couldn't help asking, 'Who's Mrs Todd?'

'Ah . . .' Mrs Jenkins' eyes gleamed with satisfaction. 'I thought you wouldn't know about *her*! New to the village, and a right bold minx she is, an' all. "Hello, Mrs J," she says the first time she comes in here. "You can call me a merry divorcee—and I promise to give you lots of lovely gossip!" Dang cheek, talking to me like that!'

Alicia had difficulty in keeping a straight face. It sounded as if Mrs Jenkins had well and truly met her match.

'That saucy madam has a decorating shop in Shrewsbury, and Squire had her in to do some work up at the Hall. My word—he'll rue the day he let her in the house, just see if he don't!' she added with relish. 'I knows for a fact that she stays up there some nights! Right wanton she is, with her long scarlet fingernails and wearing no proper underwear— disgusting, I call it! Oh yes, I knows what she's after. Got a fancy to be the second Mrs Ratcliffe, she has, and no mistake! I reckons she'll succeed, too—if someone don't come along to spoil that trollop's little game . . .'

Alicia turned around to see Mrs Jenkins eyeing her hopefully. 'I really don't think that Mr Ratcliffe's and Mrs Todd's relationship is any of our business, do you?' she said coldly, pleased to note the obvious disappointment and chagrin in the other woman's face. 'Now, I'm in a hurry to get back, so could you put everything in a box, and then I'll be on my way?'

Alicia drove the short journey back to the farm, a

prey to conflicting emotions. She'd always known that Mrs Jenkins was a wicked old gossip; however, it seemed as if the newcomer to the village, the 'merry divorcee', had her measure. And if Mrs Todd was half as tough as Mrs Jenkins obviously thought she was, then Giles and his new girl-friend were obviously made for each other! Not that it was any of her business what went on up at the Hall. If Giles wanted to have yet another of his rip-roaring affairs, this time with someone who sounded like a cross between Jezebel and Mae West he might well need his head examined, but it was—thank God!—absolutely nothing to do with her. It had taken her years to come to terms with the disillusionment and betrayal she had experienced at his hands. She now knew herself to have been nothing more than a victim of an adolescent sickness; the fact that she had once thought it to be a terminal illness only went to show how stupidly young and innocent she had been. Thank goodness she was now so much older, and well in control of her emotions.

Oh yes? What about last night? The question, rising deep from her subconscious, seemed every bit as unanswerable now as it had yesterday. It was . . . well . . . 'It was nothing but a ghastly mistake,' she muttered aloud. Giles was just being his usual randy self, and as for her . . .? She honestly didn't know why she'd responded the way she had, but she did know that it *definitely* was never going to happen again!

'Hi! How you can face driving that rubbish bin on wheels beats me!' Polly called out as she drove into the farmyard. 'I've seen Elsie. She's had the doctor out, and although she's feeling lousy, she said to tell you that she thinks she's going to live. I've also managed to get more water troughs for the sheep into the barn, but there seems to be a blockage in the pipe somewhere, so I've called out a plumber. It's all

go today, isn't it? By the way, Giles Ratcliffe called
by, and . . .'

'What on earth was he doing here?' Alicia asked
sharply, getting out of the Land Rover.

'Well, actually, I'm not entirely sure,' the younger
girl shrugged. 'He did mention something about
looking around the farm to assess it for new tenants,
I think. But he seemed much more interested in your
age!'

'My age . . .?'

'I know—it's daft, isn't it? It took me some time to
persuade him that you're really twenty-four. For some
reason he seemed convinced that you were a year
younger than you are. Anyway, we had a very cosy
cup of coffee in the kitchen, and I must say that he
was very friendly—quite a smooth charmer, in fact.'

Alicia gave a harsh bark of laughter. 'Oh, yes?
Giles being charming means Giles wants something—
I hope you counted the spoons after he left.'

'Wow! You've really got your knife into him,
haven't you!' Polly looked at her with startled eyes.
'But I thought—I mean, when I saw Elsie just now,
she said that you and he were once wildly in love,
and . . .'

'Elsie talks a lot of nonsense. It's time she learnt to
mind her own damned business!' Alicia retorted
curtly. 'Now, for goodness' sake, help me to get
everything out of the Land Rover, before we both
freeze to death.'

'Okay, okay!' muttered Polly, opening the back of
the vehicle and lifting out a large box. 'Oh, by the
way,' she added, 'I hope I'm allowed to mention that
the electricity man called to read the meter—or did I
take a liberty inviting him into the house, as well?'

Alicia sighed. 'I'm sorry. It's just that . . .'

'. . . you don't want to talk about, or have anything
to do with, Giles Ratcliffe? Okay—message received
and understood.' Polly grinned as she hauled out
another box. 'If the Wicked Squire should happen to

call on us sweet young maidens again, I'll try and
remember to slam the door firmly in his face!'

'You do that!' Alicia gave her a bleak smile.

'Dare I ask what we're having for lunch?' Polly
asked as they entered the kitchen.

'Certainly you may. We're going to have bread,
cheese and pickles. I've decided to spend the afternoon
teaching myself to cook, and I'm planning to produce
something—although I'm not quite sure exactly what—
for an early supper tonight. And anyone who makes
stupid jokes about the need for indigestion tablets,'
Alicia added darkly, 'will be sent to their room with
dry bread and water.'

'Hey, this is really great!' Polly enthused some six
hours later as she helped herself to another slice of
lemon meringue pie. 'I knew you were kidding about
not being able to cook.'

Alicia put down her fork with a sigh. 'I wasn't, you
know. It's taken me all afternoon just to produce this
meal. I never realised just how much work goes into
producing even the simplest food—I shall have to
give Mrs Simpson and Elsie an immediate rise in
salary!'

'Well, I think you should give yourself a pat on the
back. Those chops and the onions in white sauce
were absolutely delicious.'

'What loyalty!' Alicia teased. 'However, since
your're being so complimentary, I'll freely admit that
I nearly had hysterics when I couldn't find any
cookery books.' She began to clear the plates from
the table. 'It was only when, in sheer desperation, I
was hunting through the bookcase in the office, that I
came across an ancient, handwritten recipe book.
Luckily, it seems to have been written for amateurs
like myself, but it took me ages to read the spidery
writing.'

Polly's eyes sparkled with interest as Alicia placed
the small brown leather book in her hands. 'I'll tell
you what,' she said, after looking through the pages

which were stained yellow with age. 'If you're going
to do the cooking, how about my translating the
recipes for you?'

'It's a bargain,' Alicia agreed. 'Now we've got to
hurry and get the washing up done, because we still
haven't put up all the wattle hurdles for the sheep. I
hope you're feeling fit, because when I looked in the
barn an hour ago, some of those ewes looked as if
they were going to produce their lambs any minute
now. And if so, that means we've got a long hard
night ahead of us.'

And how right I was! Alicia thought glancing at
her watch as she sank down on a bale of straw. It
was half past ten, and this was the first opportunity
she'd had to take a break since they'd come into the
barn after supper. Pouring herself some hot coffee
from a thermos, she knew that if she'd felt tired last
night, it was nothing to the way her bones and
muscles were aching now. Polly hadn't realised exactly
what was involved with lambing, but when she'd sent
her off to bed an hour ago, the girl had been almost
grey with fatigue and exhaustion.

Not only had they the task of setting up the
hurdles, with which to pen the ewes into small groups
for ease of handling, but three of the sheep had
decided to give birth to lambs while all this had been
going on. One of the ewes had even produced twins,
to Polly's great excitement. And then, as if it was
contagious, the sheep had begun dropping their lambs
thick and fast. They had both been kept so busy that
there had been hardly time to talk as they checked
over each new arrival, making sure that as soon as
they could move, the mothers and their offspring
were pulled out and put into separate pens.

Despite the aches and pains in her body, Alicia felt
extraordinarily euphoric. She hadn't realised, during
all those years in London, just how much she had
missed the farm and the sense of achievement that
came from helping new life into the world. But

where there was life, there was also death; and while most of the sheep had settled down for the night, the poor ewe at her feet had been struggling and straining to give birth to her lamb for the past hour.

Alicia bit her lip in indecision as she desperately tried to think of what she could do to help the animal, who was clearly nearing the point of physical exhaustion. Should she call out the vet, just for this one sheep? It was a long way for him to come at this time of night, especially since he'd already been out to the farm when there'd been no need for his services. And what if the lamb was born before he arrived? She'd feel every bit as foolish as Polly, at calling him out on a wild goose chase . . .

The sheep gave a pathetic, low bleat and she knelt down to give it some water. A moment later she almost jumped out of her skin with shock, giving a high-pitched shriek of alarm as she felt a hand grip her shoulder.

'For God's sake . . . !' she gasped, sagging back against a straw bale as she gazed up at Giles' tall figure. 'What on earth do you think you're doing, giving me a fright like that?'

'I telephoned to see how you were getting on and, not getting a reply, I thought I ought to come over and see if you were having any problems—as I can see you are!'

'Nothing that I can't handle,' she said quickly.

'Really?' he drawled, shrugging his broad shoulders out of his snow-covered waterproof jacket, before proceeding to strip off a thick jumper and roll up the sleeves of his checked shirt.

'Now hang on a minute . . .' she said breathlessly, her heart still hammering from the fright he'd given her. 'What about your own animals?' she added, edging away as he squatted down beside her.

'We've more or less finished lambing, and when I checked an hour ago, my shepherd had everything well under control,' he murmured as he concentrated on examining the panting ewe. 'It looks as if that lamb's in the breech position, and we'll have to be quick if we're going to save both it and the mother.'

'What guarantee have I got that you won't kill them instead?' she exclaimed helplessly, trying to control her ragged breathing and refusing to admit, even to herself, just how disturbing she found his close proximity.

'If something isn't done immediately, they're both as good as dead, anyway.' Giles' voice was brutally hard. 'So why don't you just shut up, Alicia, and let me get on with doing what I can for the poor animal, hmm?'

CHAPTER FIVE

'THERE you are,' Giles said, putting the small, damp bundle into Alicia's arms. 'It seems that mother and son are both alive and kicking, after all.' He stood up, stretching his tall, rangy figure before going over to wash his hands in a nearby water trough.

'Have you got any soap, and something I can use for a towel?' he asked, looking around the barn.

'Yes, I won't be a minute,' she said, laying the new-born lamb down in some fresh straw. 'I really ought to move this ewe, but I don't know whether she's capable of walking anywhere at the moment. What do you think?' she asked, extracting the items he had asked for from the large wooden box she had packed before leaving the house.

'I'd leave the poor old thing alone for tonight. She's had quite a battering, and I'm afraid there's always a chance she might not survive. Time enough to move her in the morning.'

'Yes, well, I suppose I ought to thank you for your help,' Alicia muttered uneasily.

They had both been so busy, working together as a team to save the ewe and her lamb, that she had almost forgotten that it was Giles beside her. Almost—but not quite. And now, the job completed, she found herself at a loss what to say. Her normal poise seemed to disappear whenever she was in close proximity to this man. Here in the barn, with its dim lighting and long dark shadows, she found herself feeling confused and disorientated, assailed by forces that appeared to be completely beyond her control.

82

'Don't strain yourself, Alicia,' he drawled sardonically as he towelled himself dry, before rolling down his shirt sleeves over his bare, muscular forearms. 'You knows how us h'ignorant peasant yokels be right glad to have the honour of a-serving the gentry. Especially them as is rich and comely as what you be!'

'Ha, ha—very funny!' she ground out. In any other circumstances she might have laughed at his accurate interpretation of the local dialect. But with Giles looking down at her as he slowly did up his cuff-links, his eyes roaming over her slim figure in a deliberately thorough, insolent appraisal, she realised that she had completely lost her sense of humour. 'Satisfied?' she asked bitterly.

His grey eyes gleamed with amusement. 'No,' he said, and before she realised his intention, he had pulled the combs from the knot at the top of her head, releasing the heavy mass of ash-blonde hair to fall tumbling down in a silky cloak about her shoulders.

'How—how dare you?' she gasped angrily.

Giles laughed. '*Now* I'm satisfied. Now you look more like the girl I remember.'

'Remember? Just what do you remember, I wonder?' her voice grated angrily. 'I was nothing but a pushover. Just one of a long line of conquests in your amorous career, wasn't I?' she accused him bleakly.

His dark brows jerked together over eyes suddenly hard and stormy. 'My "amorous career" . . .? What are you talking about?'

'Your dear fiancée made the position very clear, the last time I had the dubious pleasure of seeing her. Not that I knew she was your fiancée, of course. Or about all your other "girl-friends"—oh, dear me, no!' Alicia gave a shrill laugh. 'Poor Camilla, I never thought I'd feel sorry for her. But having to put up with your constant infidelities—well, no wonder she couldn't hack married life to the local stud!'

'The *what*?' With one furious stride forward, Giles had her by the shoulders. 'What in the hell would you know—or even care—about my married life?' he snarled, shaking her violently as he glared down into her dazed blue eyes, his face dark with rage.

'L-leave m-me alone!' she cried hoarsely, trying to twist away from the fingers gripping her like steel talons.

'My God! That's exactly what I should have done! Left you severely alone. And if you hadn't lied to me, I would *never* have made such a monumental fool of myself, with either you or Jed,' he said bitterly.

'You must be out of your mind!' she gasped. 'I never lied to you.'

Giles gave a harsh, derisory laugh. 'Oh, no? What about your claim to be eighteen, for instance?'

'I . . .' Alicia's cheeks burned. How foolish she'd been; how pathetically eager to appear to be grown up and sophisticated by adding just over a year to her age, during that summer long ago. It hadn't seemed very wrong at the time—it had only been a few months until her seventeenth birthday.

The anger seemed to drain away from his rigid figure, as he slowly and deliberately wound his fingers into the shining mass of her hair. 'You're quite right,' he muttered. 'I've been out of my mind for a long, long time.'

Alicia stiffened, all her senses screaming a warning as she registered the oddly thick, husky note in his voice. She mustn't make the same mistake as she had last night! Struggling to escape, she realised it was too late as Giles pulled her closer, his fingers tightening in her hair and holding her firmly imprisoned against him.

'Let me go!' she hissed, desperately trying to ignore the frightening mixture of emotions racing through her veins. She was fleetingly aware of fear, tension and panic, but as his dark head came slowly and inexorably down towards her, she was shocked to discover that she was instinctively responding to the hard warmth of his body. Hot shivers of sexual excitement gripped her stomach as she trembled against him, aware that the rapid pounding of her heart was beating in unison with his. 'No . . .!' she whispered helplessly as his mouth possessed hers, the relentless pressure forcing her lips apart, and her protest became an inaudible moan as she surrendered to the fierce intensity of his kiss.

Still holding her head firmly beneath him, he disentangled one hand from her hair, sliding it slowly down over her body to seek and find the soft curve of her breast, his fingers brushing over the hard burgeoning peak and causing a fierce tremor of pleasure to flare through her trembling figure.

'Alicia . . .!' She hardly heard the ragged groan as Giles' mouth left hers, his lips feathering down over the long curve of her throat to seek the softly scented hollows at the base of her neck, murmuring thick words of pleasure as his hand moved over her hips, moulding her soft body more closely to his. Trapped and enmeshed in a dizzy haze of feverish excitement, it was only when he slid his hand beneath her woollen shirt, sweeping it up over her silky skin to take possession of the aroused swell of her breast, that reality began to penetrate the erotic mists of desire which had her in thrall.

Oh, God! She had to stop this . . . she couldn't— she mustn't fall into the self-same trap he had set for her eight years ago. The fear and panic that she was, once again, making one of the greatest mistakes of her life gave her the strength to push Giles away.

He let her go, leaning silently against one of the old wooden pillars of the barn, and watching her efforts to compose herself with inscrutable grey eyes. 'It would appear that matters—as always where you and I are concerned—seem to have got rather out of control,' he drawled, in a bland voice devoid of all expression.

That's putting it mildly! she thought, avoiding his eye as she feverishly hunted amongst the straw bales for her combs. It wasn't until he gave a short bark of sardonic laughter that she realised she had spoken aloud.

'I agree!' His lips twisted in a wry grimace. 'Of course this isn't the time or place, but we do have a great deal to talk about, Alicia, don't we?'

She didn't answer him, concentrating on trying to pile the long length of her hair back on top of her head. Unfortunately, she couldn't seem to control her hands, which were shaking as if she was in the grip of a fever. Perhaps she was, she thought hysterically. First last night—and now, here again in the barn . . . It was only too evident that the passage of time had done nothing to diminish his overwhelming attraction for her. She really must pull herself together, and somehow try to get out of this extremely fraught, embarrassing situation with at least some semblance of dignity and composure.

'I really don't think we have anything to talk about,' she said at last, giving him what she hoped looked like a casual, uninterested shrug.

'Don't you? Surely there are so many topics of conversation for discussion between us?' he drawled. 'Among which, of course, there are some really quite riveting items, such as your late husband and my ex-wife—to name but two! So maybe you would like to come and have dinner with me, tomorrow night?' he added, not bothering to hide the steely menace behind his invitation.

Come into my parlour, said the spider to the fly . . .? Not likely! Alicia told herself, striving to deliberately blank out all expression from her face. Where did he think she'd been for the last eight years—in a nunnery? During her marriage, and especially during this last year since Walter's death, there had been many such propositions. She had been under no illusions then, and she certainly wasn't now. Besides, even if she gave Giles the benefit of the doubt, and believed that he only wanted to talk about the past— that was a topic that she definitely wished to avoid. And with his past record, he was hardly likely to keep the evening to just talk, was he? If she was going to be quite frank with herself, she didn't honestly trust her own emotions, certainly not as far as he was concerned. Their passionate encounter just now . . . well, it was bound to have given him *quite* the wrong idea. Anyway, knowing Giles, the swine probably had his latest girl-friend, the 'merry divorcee', tucked up in his bed and keeping it nice and warm for him, right this very minute!

'Well?' Giles asked laconically as he bent down to pick up his jacket.

'Thank you for the invitation, but I'm afraid I have a previous appointment,' she said firmly.

'Oh, yes? Who with?'

The damned man, why couldn't he just accept a polite refusal? 'These sheep, of course,' she muttered, gesturing around the barn.

'That's no problem. We'll have finished lambing tonight, and so my shepherd can come and look after your animals.' There was just a suspicion of laughter in his voice, reinforced by the mocking glint in his grey eyes.

Alicia sighed. There was no way she was going to get rid of him—out of this barn and out of her life— without having to be brutally frank. 'Look, Giles, there is absolutely no point in carrying on this little farce any longer. While I'm very grateful for the help you've given me with the sheep, both yesterday and tonight, I must make it clear that I have no intention of having dinner with you tomorrow—or any other night, for that matter. What happened just now . . .' She shrugged her shoulders helplessly. 'Let's just say

that it was a ghastly mistake, and leave it at that,
shall we?'

'Oh, no!' He strode swiftly across the cobbled floor
of the barn, grabbing her arm and violently swinging
her around to face him. 'Who are you trying to fool,
Alicia?' he demanded angrily. 'You know you wanted
me a few minutes ago—every bit as much as I wanted
you. So don't try and deny it!'

She flushed, shutting her eyes for a moment against
the hard, determined expression of the face so close
to her own. 'No, I—I'm not going to deny it,' she
murmured huskily. 'But it was nothing but a—a
sexual response. You are, after all, an attractive
man . . .'

'Thanks!' he snarled bitterly. 'Behave like that with
all the "attractive" men you meet, do you?'

'No! Of course not, I . . .' She bit her lip as she
saw the trap into which she had fallen. 'All right,
Giles, if you want plain speaking: the fact is that
whatever there was once between us, it's now dead
and gone. And even if it wasn't,' she added quickly
as he opened his mouth to speak, 'I definitely do *not*
want to renew a relationship that caused me nothing
but grief and pain. Got the message?'

'The message I get from you is a somewhat
contradictory one,' he drawled softly, lifting his hand
to run a finger gently over her mouth, and on down
her throat to where a rapidly beating pulse betrayed
her inner agitation. 'Your lips may say one thing, my
darling Alicia, but your body says quite another!'

'I'm not your darling!' she hissed through gritted
teeth. 'By all accounts, it's the "merry divorcee"
who's top of your pops this week!'

He raised his eyebrows. 'Melanie Todd?'

Alicia's cheeks flamed. Why on earth had she
brought up the subject of his current mistress? It was
nothing to do with her—nothing at all.

He studied her face intently for a moment, and
then gave a lazy smile. 'Well, well. Now I wonder

where you heard about Melanie . . .? He paused.
'Ah—of course! Who else but that old witch, Mrs
Jenkins? Been stirring her cauldron again, has she?'

She shrugged. 'Quite frankly, Giles, I'm simply not
interested in your love life.'

'Are you quite sure of that?' He grinned, ignoring
her attempt to escape his firm grip, as he pulled her
closer. 'Do you know, I could have sworn you were
displaying a streak of green, feminine jealousy, just
now.'

'My God! You're quite unbelievable!' she panted
breathlessly. 'Nothing but an arrogant male chauvinist
pig! Let me go—and then get the hell out of my
barn!'

'But it's not your barn, is it? Have you forgotten
that the farmhouse and the farmland belong to me?'
he drawled smoothly. 'You are merely the temporary
tenant, and I fully intend to claim back my land—just
as I fully intend to have you, too, Alicia!' he taunted,
swiftly lowering his head to brush his mouth over
hers. 'That's a promise!' he breathed thickly against
her lips, before abruptly letting her go.

'You? Have me . . .? Not till hell freezes over, you
won't!' she snarled, white-faced and shaking with
anger. 'Now, get out of here, before I call the police
and have you forcibly removed!'

'Tsk, tsk.' He shook his head in mock sorrow.
'Where are you going to find the police at this time
of night? This isn't London, you know!' he laughed
as he walked away towards the large door of the
barn. 'However, since I'm a local magistrate, maybe I
can offer you my—er—services, hmm?'

'Get out!' she screamed, almost beside herself with
rage.

He opened the door, giving her an infuriatingly
cheery wave before he disappeared into the darkness
of the night. Almost numb with tiredness and
exhaustion, Alicia sank down on a loose pile of straw,
leaning against the sheep who was now sleeping

peacefully after being the cause of so much anxiety
earlier in the evening. Perhaps it was reaction
from the nervous tension, but she was suddenly
overwhelmed by a storm of helpless tears, which
flowed down over her cheeks to splash on to the
sheep's thick, woolly coat.

At sixteen she had been fiercely independent and
defiant of Jed's authority, head over heels in love
with Giles and, most fatal of all, totally innocent of
the complexities of human behaviour. 'Green as grass
you are, and no mistake!' Elsie had said, and although
Alicia hadn't listened to her at the time, there was no
doubt that the old housekeeper had been absolutely
right.

If Giles found her patent adoration an irritant, he
gave no indication as day after day, he casually
welcomed her company as he rode about his estate.
It was July, and the hay-making was in full swing,
when Jed twisted his ankle and was confined to the
house. Giles had sent two of his men over to help
with the final stacking in the dutch barn, situated in
one of the far meadows of Winterfloods Farm.
Arriving to inspect their work at the end of one late
afternoon he had found that Alicia, resting from the
hard manual labour, had fallen fast asleep on a loose
pile of hay. It was perhaps inevitable that, when she
woke to find him lounging beside her, she should
have sleepily turned towards him, relishing the
strength of his arms as they closed about her slim
figure, and ardently welcoming the fierce, determined
possession of his lips and his body.

However hard she had tried during the subsequent
years, she had never been able to hide from herself
the fact that, innocent and ignorant of lovemaking as
she was, her desire had been every bit as strong as
his, the feverish intensity of her response an irresistible
enticement, overwhelming any scruples he might have
had. She could never forget the passion that exploded

between them every time they managed to be alone, during the following two weeks.

Jed, of course, had eventually discovered the truth, and the subsequent blazing row between them had been the last time she had seen or spoken to her stepfather. Her threat to leave the farm had sprung more from anger than serious intent, but the events of the following day had caused her to translate her angry words into serious action.

Locked in her room for the rest of the day, she had finally managed to escape late the next morning, when Jed had gone off in his tractor to one of the far meadows. Although she had hunted high and low, Giles was nowhere to be found. Finally, desperate to see him, she had called at Eastdale Hall, only to meet Camilla Harrison, who informed her that she had been engaged to Giles for the past year, and that they would be getting married in a few months' time.

'I'm always having to get rid of silly little girls like you,' Camilla had said with a harsh laugh. 'You've got to hand it to Giles, he certainly believes in the *droit de seigneur*!'

Shocked and stunned, almost out of her mind with wretched misery, Alicia had returned to the farm, and throwing some clothes into a suitcase, she had hitched a lift from a lorry passing the end of the lane. She'd had no idea of what she intended to do when she reached London, but in the event she had found a job working in the kitchen of a large hotel. She had only been there for some three months when fate, in the shape of a young girl absentmindedly crossing a busy road, had changed her life for ever. She didn't remember very much of what Sir Walter Preston had called her 'outstanding act of bravery' in saving his daughter's life. And even when she had fully recovered her health and her bones had mended, she remained oddly apathetic, though deeply grateful for Polly and her father's warm care and attention.

It was Sir Walter's proposal of marriage which had

jerked her back to the real world. 'You've become a real favourite with my daughter,' he had said, his North Country accent coming to the fore as it did in moments of stress and emotion. 'I know that I've neglected the girl, but I don't aim to do so in the future. However, it seems that she can't do without you and neither, I reckon, can I. So, I think it best we get married. Oh yes,' he had added, 'I know there's been someone else—with your looks it stands to reason there would be—but if he weren't no good, then you have no need to worry that I won't look after you properly, because I shall. And unless you've a mind to it, there's no call to feel you have to share my bedroom either. You and I—well, we're a case of December and May, and I hope I've enough sense to know that I'm not a young girl's dream hero.'

Knowing that Giles was lost to her for ever, Alicia had married Walter Preston, and it had been a decision she had never regretted. A few months after they were married, he had been anxious and depressed about a business deal, and she had taken him to her room that night, solely for comfort and consolation. That, too, was a decision she had never regretted, and if Walter's lovemaking had failed to touch her emotionally, nevertheless their marriage had been a very peaceful and contented one. She had been determined to make Walter and Polly happy, and she knew that as far as was humanly possible she had succeeded.

By the time Walter died, she had grown to love him dearly. He had left her very rich indeed, but she would gladly have traded every penny to have him back, sorely missing his sound advice and wise counsel.

Over the years, her feelings for Giles had been deeply buried, and if it hadn't been for Jed's unexpected death, she would never have returned to Eastdale. She would never have had to see Giles again, and could have kept her emotions permanently under control.

But now . . .? Once more, she had only to be near him and she had become lost to all time and place. She had once again fallen a victim to his overwhelming, sensual masculinity, melting in his arms as she had all those years ago. He seemed to have cast a magic spell over her, but it was black magic, and she wanted none of it.

'Oh, Walter, why did you have to go and leave me?' she moaned, burying her face in the sheep's fleece.

Eventually realising that she couldn't stay here in the barn all night, she gave a heavy sigh and went to check that the ewes and their lambs were settled down, before turning off the lights and making her way back across the snow-covered yard to the farmhouse.

Alicia woke up the next morning to find that she had overslept. Ten o'clock! She struggled to sit up, overcome by guilt at having neglected the animals, who must be starving by now. Brushing her long fair hair back from her brow, she saw that there was a mug of tea beside the clock, with a piece of paper propped up beside it.

Your turn to lie in! Polly had written. *I'll see to feeding the calves and sheep—so go back to sleep!*

With a smile, Alicia settled back against the pillows. The tea was cold by now, of course, but it was a typically kind, thoughtful gesture by Polly. She was so lucky to have the bright, amusing girl for a stepdaughter. Not only was she one of the easiest people to live with, but her warm and lively personality meant that their life together was seldom dull.

The clear, morning light flooding into the bedroom was helping to banish last night's dark shadows from her mind. Looking at matters calmly and

logically, she had to face the fact that she was
always going to be attracted to Giles. There was a
basic chemistry between them, that fused into quite
another element whenever they became close to
one another: a raw, hungry sensuality that had
them both in thrall. It seemed that her absence
from the farm had done nothing to diminish the
fundamental attraction they felt for each other,
merely damping down the flames which had needed
only the fuel of their renewed contact to be ignited
again into a raging inferno. The answer to the
problem was therefore a simple one: she must leave
the farm and go back to London as soon as possible.

Giles wasn't going to put any obstacle in her way,
she reminded herself as she threw back the covers,
slipping out of bed to go over to stare out of the
window at the farmyard and the snow-covered fields
beyond. He was obviously intending to take back
and manage the farm . . . her lips tightened at the
recollection of what he'd said last night. Well, if he
thought he was going to get his hands on *her*, he
was definitely going to be disappointed! How could
he possibly imagine that she'd make the same
mistake twice—let alone join the long list of women
with whom he'd had affairs? Not only was he clearly
out of his head, but his arrogance and conceit was
truly unbelievable!

The sound of a boot scraping on cobbles distracted
her, and she glanced down to see a strange man
walking around the farmyard with a clipboard in his
hand. Frowning, she tried to think who it could be
as she hurried into a new pair of dark brown cord
trousers, completing her working ensemble by
putting on a cream woollen shirt and a heavy Aran
pullover. It could be a man from the Ministry, of
course, she thought as she quickly drew a brush
through her long hair before hurrying downstairs
and out into the yard. She'd been out of touch with
the machinations of the Ministry of Agriculture for

so long that she could be inadvertently contravening some important regulation.

'Can I help you?' she asked the man, who she now saw was unlikely to have come from any Ministry. He looked more like one of Polly's vacuous friends, she thought, her eyes running quickly over the expensive cavalry-twill trousers, and the Barbour jacket that was *de rigueur* among the county set.

'No, I don't think so, actually,' he drawled, barely giving her a quick glance as he continued to make notes on his clipboard.

'Then may I please know who you are, and what you're doing here?' she enquired, deciding that it wouldn't be too difficult to find herself actively disliking this man, who was walking around the yard as if he owned it.

He sighed impatiently. 'If it's any business of yours, which I am quite sure it's not, my name is Nigel Verney-Browne . . .'

'Browne with an "E", of course!' she murmured.

His thin mouth tightened with annoyance as he registered the trace of irony in her voice. 'Yes. For your information,' he sneered, 'I am a partner in Smith, Garratt and Robinson. The well known land agents,' he added patiently, as if talking to a particularly dim-witted child. 'We act for Mr Ratcliffe, for whom I am assessing the curtilage of the farmhouse and buildings. And now, if you don't mind, I would like to get on with my work, Miss . . .?'

'Lady Preston,' Alicia snapped, gritting her teeth against a rising tide of anger at the man's arrant rudeness, and his casual dismissal of her presence. 'And I do mind,' she said coldly. 'This is still my farm, and until I relinquish the tenancy I expect—if nothing else—a modicum of politeness from Mr Ratcliffe's land agents.'

'Really, madam . . .'

'I suggest that you go back to your employers,' she said, ignoring his interruption. 'What was their name? Sue, Grabbit and Runne . . .? Kindly tell them to have the courtesy to make an appointment the next time they wish to see me. You can also tell them that you, Mr Verney-Brown-with-an-"e", are definitely *persona non grata* as far as I am concerned. Goodbye!'

'Really, Miss—er—Lady Preston, I'm sorry if . . .'

'So am I,' she said curtly. 'Now, I have no intention of prolonging this conversation any further. I want you in your car and off my property. Hurry up!' she snapped as he stood goggling at her. 'I can see no reason why I should catch frost-bite standing out here and wasting my time with you. So, start moving. Or do I have to go and fetch a shotgun?'

'Ah . . . no . . . I mean . . . yes, of course, I'm just leaving. Yes, indeed,' he muttered, turning to hurry away back to his car with as much dignity as he could muster.

'Bravo, Ally!' laughed Polly as she came out from behind the cowshed door. 'I nearly split my sides listening to you giving him what for!'

'Umm . . .' Alicia frowned as she watched the land agent's car disappearing into the distance. 'I shouldn't have been so rude, of course, but he was so damn condescending that I'm afraid I completely lost my temper.'

'What was he doing here, anyway?'

'He said he was measuring the house and the barns. I'm not sure what it's all about, but maybe I'd better give my solicitor a ring? Incidentally, I haven't said how much I appreciated being allowed to sleep in this morning. Bless you, love,' she gave the girl a kiss on the cheek. 'Brr, it's freezing out here. Why don't we go inside and have a hot cup of coffee, and then I'll give you a hand with the sheep.'

'There's no need for either of us to do anything—

sheepwise!' Polly grinned, stamping her cold feet. 'Mr Bates has arrived and is now in charge of the barn—or so he tells me.'

Alicia looked at her in surprise. 'Old Tom Bates? The shepherd at Hall Farm? What on earth is he doing here?'

'But surely . . .? Surely you knew that Giles Ratcliffe was sending him over to look after our sheep for us?'

'Oh, lord! I'd quite forgotten that Giles did mention something about it last night, but . . .'

'Last night?' Polly raised her eyebrows.

A tide of colour burned across Alicia's cheeks. 'He—he just happened to call by, when I was out in the barn with the sheep,' she muttered.

'Ho!'

'Ho—nothing!' Alicia retorted quickly, before striding off towards the large stone barn.

The old shepherd looked up, his weatherbeaten face creasing into a broad smile as she pushed open the heavy oak door. 'How do, Miss Alicia. We's all uncommon glad to have you back at the farm, and no mistake.'

'It's very kind of you to help me out like this, Tom. It's been a long time since I was involved with sheep at lambing time.'

'The guv'nor said as how he reckoned you could do with a hand, now that we's finished up at the Hall.' He bent down to settle a new-born lamb closer to its mother.

'Is everything all right?' she asked, bringing over a pail of water to fill a nearby water trough.

'Well, there's one or two of them ewes what I'm not too happy about, but all in all, I'd say you've done a good job.'

From old Tom Bates, that was praise indeed! Alicia smiled at the shepherd. 'You will let me know if you need anything, won't you?'

'That I will. Now, you just be a-leaving everything

to me from now on, Miss Alicia. You knows full well them sheep is now in good hands.'

She hid a grin as she realised that she was being kindly but firmly dismissed. Tom Bates was like an old-fashioned nanny; he liked to be left in complete control to look after his charges, without any outside interference.

'Isn't Mr Bates a darling?' Polly enthused when she returned to the house. 'He gave me some jolly good tips about how and when to dip the sheep, and what to do about warble flies in the summer.'

'Well, I'm sure that was fascinating information, and might be useful if we were going to be here in the summer. But since we'll be returning to live happily in London any day now . . .' Alicia shrugged.

'I know—I know,' Polly muttered. 'But I do wish it was possible to stay on at the farm.' She hesitated for a moment. 'If you want the truth, I haven't been all that happy in London. In fact, I've been pretty fed up with the whole scene for some time now. No, no . . .' she added hastily, 'it's nothing to do with you, or our life together—that's fine. It's just . . . well, rattling around that big house, trying all sorts of jobs and being no good at any of them, the endless parties where I've met the same people every time . . . it's all become so damn boring!'

'I never knew . . .' Alicia looked at her with dismay. 'Why on earth didn't you tell me you felt that way?'

Polly shrugged. 'I kept hoping something would turn up, I suppose. And so it has—in a roundabout way! I've only been here at Winterfloods for a few days, and yet I already love the place. I know you'll say I'm out of my mind,' she grinned ruefully at Alicia. 'But I now know *exactly* what I want to do, which is to live in the country and run a farm. And before you start laughing,' she added quickly, 'I was talking on the phone to Bob, earlier this morning. He says there's no reason why, if I'm still of the same mind in the autumn, I can't try for a place at the Royal Agricultural College in Cirencester. And that's precisely what I have every intention of doing!'

'Goodness, Polly! I—I don't know what to say . . .'

Her stepdaughter shrugged. 'There's no need to say anything. Only time is going to prove to you that I'm serious about farming. But since we haven't anything vitally urgent on the agenda at home, why can't we stay on up here for a bit? And even if you feel you have to get back, you don't need me, do you? I'd much prefer to remain here at Winterfloods, and I could keep an eye on things for you, couldn't I?' she added eagerly.

'I . . . I don't know . . .' Alicia brushed a distracted hand through her hair. She had no real objections about staying on at the farm for a while—other than wishing to get away from Giles, of course. However, that was something she really didn't feel that she wanted to go into with Polly . . . she gazed at the younger girl who was regarding her with a determined set to her chin. How extraordinary—she'd never in a million years have thought that Polly would be interested in farming. Of course, the girl was very like her father. When Walter had set his mind on something, he ruthlessly pursued his way towards his objective, never letting anything stand in his way . . .

'Well . . .?'

'Hold on!' Alicia protested. 'It's not just a matter of your future career—although I do hope that you'll think hard and long about it, Polly. There are . . . well, there are a lot of other factors involved. I can't possibly take a decision just like that,' she snapped her fingers. 'I'd have to give the whole matter some considerable thought.'

'Would it help if you had a long weekend on your own in which to do your thinking?'

Alicia sighed. 'What are you up to now?'

'Well, Bob has got a long weekend free, and he's invited me to go and stay at his cousin's large farm, over the border in Wales. I did say that I couldn't make it—after all, we've both been working flat out looking after all the animals. But, now that you've got Mr Bates seeing to the sheep . . . and if you could manage the cows on your own . . .?'

'Of course I can. You've been a great help, and it's time you had a break.'

'Are you sure?'

'Positive,' Alicia said firmly. 'I've been putting off going through the farm accounts, which Mr Pemberton is going to need, to settle Jed's affairs. And I can also practise my new hobby of cooking, and not have to worry if a dish turns out to be inedible! Go along,' she added as Polly stood looking at her hesitantly. 'You'd better give him a ring and say you can make it after all.'

Waving Polly and the vet off after lunch—Bob looking somewhat dazed as he climbed into the Ferrari which Polly had insisted on driving—Alicia suddenly remembered Mr Verney-Browne. It might be a good idea to give her solicitor a ring, and check up on whether she'd really been within her rights in ordering the ghastly man off the farm.

'*He's what?*' she shrieked ten minutes later, jumping up from her chair and pacing agitatedly up and down in front of the desk in the office. 'What do you mean? How can Mr Ratcliffe's agents possibly serve me with a notice to quit this farm in just three weeks from now?'

'Calm down, Lady Preston. Please . . . I beg you . . . there's no need to become so . . . er . . . excited . . .' Mr Pemberton's voice trembled over the phone. 'I'm sure we can find a way to solve this matter . . .'

'We'd better!' she retorted furiously. 'That damn man was here last night, and he never said a word about what he was planning to do. I'll give him "notice to quit" . . . just see if I don't!' she ground out through clenched teeth. 'If Mr Giles-bloody-Ratcliffe thinks that he can evict me, in just three weeks' time, from a house that my family has lived in for generations—*then he's got another think coming!*'

CHAPTER SIX

FOR the rest of the afternoon, Alicia felt so full of anger and fury that she couldn't seem to settle down to any positive work, let alone studying the farm accounts as she had planned. In the end, she decided to go into the kitchen and make some bread. At least kneading the heavy dough might help to get rid of some of her nervous tension, and it was certainly going to be more productive than bellowing with rage down the phone at poor Mr Pemberton.

Not that her solicitor had been unsympathetic, although clearly shocked by her use of strong language. 'Please, Lady Preston—I beg you to calm down and restrain yourself!' he had muttered, his voice trembling with agitation. 'Believe me, I do understand how upsetting this must be for you. And I certainly agree that giving you notice to leave the farm on Lady Day which, as you say, is only three weeks away—does seem unreasonable . . . most unreasonable indeed.'

'That must be the understatement of the year!' she retorted bitterly, coming slowly off the boil and managing to find enough self-control to contain her rage at simmering point.

'Yes, it's a great pity that your dear father didn't have a son and heir,' he added sadly. 'However, I have to tell you that Mr Ratcliffe is quite within his rights. You and I, my dear Lady Preston, might well find his action somewhat hasty and unnecessarily precipitate, but Mr Ratcliffe is acting within the law, I'm afraid.'

'I bet he is!' she said grimly, relieving her feelings by violently kicking the waste paper basket across the room. 'But is there nothing I can do to gain some more time? Quite apart from anything else, three weeks is hardly long enough to sell the farm animals, and there's the matter of packing up and trying to clear everything out of the house. My family have lived here for generations, for heaven's sake!'

'Ah, yes, well . . .' he hesitated. 'Since receiving the "notice to quit" from Smith, Garrett and Robinson this morning, I have had one or two thoughts on the matter.' He coughed. 'If I understand the situation: you are willing to vacate the farm, but you would wish for more time to do so, hmm?'

'Well, yes . . . I mean, there's no way I can possibly pack up and leave here in three weeks!'

Mr Pemberton's cough echoed down the phone again. 'As you may or may not know, it is usual for land agents to deal with one another. Just as in my own case, where I would always prefer to deal directly with a fellow lawyer, so it is with other professional men. It enables us to make certain—ah—allegations and charges that would, if uttered by the protagonists in a case, cause lifelong enmity.'

There was a long pause, while Alicia gritted her teeth, repressing an urge to shout, 'Get on with it!' at the elderly solicitor. There was no doubt that Mr Pemberton believed in using twenty words when one or two would do.

'Before you rang,' he continued at last, 'I did take the liberty of contacting Mr Truscott, who is the senior partner of Truscott's, a well regarded firm of land agents in Shrewsbury, and they also have many branches throughout the country. He and I have talked briefly on the telephone, and he has made one or two suggestions which I feel might be helpful.'

Alicia frowned. 'I'm not sure I understand all this,' she said, trying to contain her impatience. 'Are you saying I ought to have another firm of land agents acting for me?'

'Precisely.'

'But what's the point? What can this Mr Truscott do for me that I can't do for myself?'

'Ah—that is the nub of the question. I am suggesting that you retain Mr Truscott's services, and instruct him to deal with Mr Ratcliffe's land agents on your behalf.'

She sighed. 'It all sounds very complicated.'

'Not at all, my dear young lady. Mr Truscott believes that it may well be possible for you to make a formal claim for the tenancy of the farm . . .'

'But I don't . . . I mean . . . I hadn't thought of . . .'

'Of course you hadn't,' the elderly solicitor agreed. 'However, Mr Ratcliffe and his agents don't know that, do they?' He gave a dry chuckle. 'Mr Truscott is of the opinion that you may well have a very good case for gaining the tenancy, such as the fact that you grew up and worked on the farm, for instance. If, therefore, Mr Truscott were to tell Mr Ratcliffe's agents, Smith, Garratt and Robinson, that you were making a claim to the farm, they would have to take the threat seriously, hmm? And that would give Mr Truscott the opportunity not only to halt the eviction order, but to bargain for a more reasonable length of time in which to enable you to vacate the property.'

'Yes, I see what you're driving at.' Alicia sat down at the desk, her lips widening in a broad smile as she realised the implications of what he was saying. 'What's more, I can also see that the threat of losing the land might well give Mr Ratcliffe a bit of a headache—and serve him right!' Her smile broadened even further at the thought. 'But why do I need Mr Truscott? Surely I can tell Mr Ratcliffe myself?'

'Oh, no, my dear young lady, that would be most unwise!' Mr Pemberton cautioned firmly. 'Matters can sometimes become very—er—very nasty and acrimonious in a case like this. Oh, dear me, yes! I would advise you, very strongly indeed, to leave the two agents to deal with one another. If they do so, then there is no reason why you and Mr Ratcliffe should not remain moderately friendly. After all, one does not want to fall out with one's local landowner and squire, does one?'

Throwing the bread dough down on to the kitchen table, thumping and kneading it for all she was worth, Alicia gave a grim laugh. A fat lot Mr Pemberton knew about anything! Quite frankly, *one* couldn't wait to bash *one's* local landowner and squire about the head with *one's* answer to his eviction order! And goodness—wouldn't Giles be hopping mad! Winterfloods Farm, with its five hundred acres of good arable land, must be worth well over half a million pounds. Not that Giles would ever sell the farm, of course, but with the threat of losing the land for up to fifty years—and more, if she married and had a son—well, he wouldn't just be mad, he'd be foaming at the mouth with rage and frustration!

Following the phone call with Mr Pemberton, she'd immediately rung Truscott's and made an appointment to see Mr Truscott tomorrow morning, explaining that it was an urgent case and time was of the essence.

And how right she was! *Three weeks!* How could Giles possibly expect her to vacate this house in that short space of time? Her family had lived here for so long that the attics must be filled to the brim with goodness knows what rubbish. Of course, he'd known that she had never intended to stay on at the farm and that she'd be going back to London when she'd found someone to look after the animals. But to act in this hasty and underhand fashion—and not even saying a word last night about what he was planning . . . well, she'd never have believed him capable of such treacherous behaviour.

Which just went to show what an idiot she was.

Once a skunk, always a skunk! she told herself as she put the dough into a large bowl, covering it with a floured cloth and setting it beside the warm stove to rise, before she went out to see the cows.

Having expended some considerable physical energy in hauling hay bales into the cowshed, Alicia returned to the kitchen in a somewhat calmer frame of mind. Kneading the risen dough, and putting it into greased bread tins, she paused as she was struck by a sudden thought. Mr Pemberton had suggested that she apply for the tenancy of the farm, merely as a device to enable her to bargain for more time to leave Winterfloods. But . . . but why should her application be only a stratagem? *Why shouldn't she apply for the tenancy—in earnest?*

Quickly placing the bread tins by the stove to prove the dough, she made herself a strong cup of coffee and then sat down at the kitchen table to consider the points at issue.

Ever since she had come back to Shropshire—albeit unwillingly—it had never occurred to her to question her eventual return to London. In fact, and especially as far as her relationship with Giles was concerned, her main consideration had been to ensure that she got away from the farm as quickly as possible.

Now she realised that it wasn't the farm itself—the house, or the land and the animals—from which she had wished to escape. Sitting here in the warm kitchen, it seemed as though for the last eight years she had been looking down the wrong end of a telescope. Winterfloods Farm and the village of Eastdale had seemed to embody all that had gone wrong with her life, whereas—in reality—it had been her unhappy life with her stepfather, and her disastrous love affair with Giles, which were the root cause of her unhappiness.

However, looking at the matter with a clearer, less jaundiced eye, quite a different picture emerged.

With Jed gone, she had been surprised to discover just how much she was enjoying herself at the farm. She was well aware that it wasn't an easy life, and she'd been brutally frank and down to earth with Polly about the trials and tribulations in working the land, and looking after animals in adverse weather conditions. No one could accuse her of being starry-eyed about the hard work involved either. Thanks to the luxury of her life in London, Alicia knew that she'd allowed herself to become soft and out of condition. During the last few days, for instance, she'd discovered some aching muscles she hadn't used for years! But as each day went by she was getting fitter, and she knew that if she decided to take the plunge, she was quite capable of running the farm. She'd need some help, of course, but there was Elsie's husband, Fred, who would soon be back to work, and she could always hire any other assistance that she might need . . .

'Hang on—don't get too carried away!' Alicia cautioned herself out loud. It would be a grave mistake to talk herself into believing that taking back and running the farm was going to be a piece of cake. Far from it! She must carefully weigh up the pros and cons—especially the cons. Quite apart from anything she might want to do, her first duty was to Polly. She'd promised Walter that she would look after his daughter, and the girl must be her first priority. However, Polly seemed to be set on training for a farming career, and while that decision might be a temporary flash in the pan, she had definitely never known her stepdaughter to be so positive about the choice of a career before. And even if she eventually changed her mind, there was no doubt that Polly seemed to enjoy living in the country. Moreover, there would be no question of giving up the London house, certainly not straight away. She could easily afford to keep both it and the farm as well, if she wanted to.

Which just left the main fly in the ointment—*Giles*. If she gained the tenancy and stayed on here at the farm, it would mean living in the same village—and having to see him regularly going about his business. How would she feel about that? She'd probably never have to meet him face to face, of course. If she was granted the tenancy, he would be so angry that it was a cast-iron certainty he'd never speak to her again. On the other hand . . .

All through the rest of the day and far into the night, Alicia wrestled with the question of whether she should seriously apply for the tenancy of the farm, the arguments swaying back and forth in her mind, first one way and then the other. It wasn't until she woke up, feeling tired and bleary-eyed, that she at last resolved the question and came to a hard and fast decision: she was going to fight for the tenancy of Winterfloods Farm.

Sitting down to a breakfast of her own delicious homemade bread and butter, she realised that despite her eight years in London, she was her father's daughter and farming was in her blood. With the clarity of hindsight she could see that all her life she had responded to outside stimuli, that she had been swept along by circumstances over which she had no control. Both Jed, and then Giles, had prompted her into flight, and she had married Walter because he had offered her a safe haven. Maybe those actions were understandable, especially when looked at in the light of just how young she'd been all those years ago; but she was now twenty-four, and she must break out of the mental strait-jacket in which she had been imprisoned. This time she would be making a positive choice, as opposed to a negative reaction and, however rightly or wrongly it turned out, it would at least be her *own* decision.

Looking up at the old pine clock on the kitchen dresser, she gave a yelp of dismay. It was all very well sitting here, busily expounding on a new philosophy of life for herself, but if she didn't get a move on and feed the cows, she was going to be late for her eleven o'clock appointment with Mr Truscott.

Going across to the cowshed, she suddenly realised that the temperature outside had risen considerably. Not only was it very much warmer, but the morning sun was already beginning to melt some of the ice on the roofs of the farm buildings.

Scrambling through the morning chores, and after having a brief word with Mr Bates, Alicia realised that she had very little time in which to get changed. Taking the stairs two at a time, she dashed into her bedroom and threw open the door of her wardrobe. A moment or two later, she realised with dismay that her blue Saint Laurent suit would have to go to the cleaner's before she could wear it again. Some form of oil, possibly from sitting on one of the drums in the back of the Land Rover, had left greasy marks on both the jacket and skirt. Having told Polly to bring up from London only warm, casual clothing, she really had no other choice than to put on the mink coat and black dress that she had worn to attend Jed's funeral.

'It's just not my day!' she shouted in frustration some minutes later as the Land Rover resolutely refused to start. Cross, hot and bothered, she went back indoors to phone the local garage.

'I can't get the damned vehicle to start!' she explained when Johnny Knight answered her call. 'Can you come down here with some jump leads?'

'You ain't the only one what's complaining this morning,' he grumbled. 'If I had five pounds for all them phone calls, I'd be rich b'now. It's the weather, see.'

'For goodness' sake, Johnny!' she gritted her teeth impatiently. 'Who cares about the weather? Can you help me—or can't you?'

'Women drivers! Now it be thawing after that there snow, your engine's damp, ain't it? Stands to reason that ol' heap ain't a-going to start. I'll be along presently, but I've got a deal of other cars to see to first of all.'

· Giving a heavy sigh, and praying for patience, Alicia put down the phone. She had said she wouldn't be seen dead in the Ferrari, but if only Polly hadn't taken it to Wales, she would have been pathetically grateful to be able to use it now. As it was, she was going to miss her appointment with Mr Truscott, and since today was Friday, she hadn't a hope of seeing him until Monday, at the earliest.

Bitterly cursing her bad luck, she had just decided to go upstairs and get changed back into her working clothes when she heard the sound of a car outside in the yard. 'Good old Johnny!' she murmured thankfully as she ran out of the house, the smile dying on her lips as she saw that it wasn't Johnny Knight.

'Wh-what are you doing here?' she demanded, viewing with deep apprehension the sight of Giles' tall figure emerging from a gunmetal grey Porsche.

'I just called by at the garage for some petrol, and Johnny told me you were in trouble. He said something about you not being able to start the Land Rover . . .?'

'Yes . . . well . . . I'm late for an appointment . . .' she muttered, fervently wishing he would go away.

'Where are you trying to get to?' he asked, leaning casually against the open door of his car. 'Not another funeral, surely?'

'What . . .?' Alicia looked at him in confusion, before she glanced down at her black dress and fur coat. 'No, I—I want . . . I mean . . . well, if you must know, I'm trying to get to Shrewsbury, and—and I can't start that foul vehicle!' She glared over at the Land Rover.

'I'm not surprised!' He laughed. 'Never mind—I'm going into Shrewsbury, so I'll be able to give you a lift. Come on—hop in,' he added, walking around to open the passenger door.

'Are you really?' she smiled, hurrying towards him, before coming to an abrupt halt as she realised that she couldn't possible be so two-faced. How could she accept a lift from the man when, in half an hour's time, she was going to be with Mr Truscott and busily plotting to take Giles' farm away from him? She might be very angry with him—and indeed she certainly was!—but to behave in that sort of perfidious, treacherous way would only brand her as every bit as deceitful as Giles himself.

'Hurry up, Alicia, we can't stand around here all day.'

'No . . . I—I don't think I can come with you. I—er . . .'

Giles swore briefly under his breath. 'A more damned stupid woman I have yet to meet . . .!' he grated, taking a swift step forward, sweeping her up in his arms and dumping her struggling figure unceremoniously into the car.

'What in hell do you think . . .?' she shouted furiously, unable to complete the sentence, the breath being driven from her body as he quickly slammed the Porsche into reverse, before turning around in the farmyard and roaring off down the lane.

'What do I think I'm doing?' Giles gave a bark of sardonic laughter as he looked at the girl lying winded against the grey leather seat. 'You wanted to go into Shrewsbury, so I'm taking you there. However, I would suggest that you fasten your seat belt, before we're stopped by a policeman.'

'If the police stop this car, it can only be for speeding!' she retorted angrily, finding her voice at last as she did up her belt. 'For God's sake, slow down—I'm not planning to die just yet!' she added, wincing as he drove round a corner on what seemed to be only two wheels.

'I can't think why you're complaining?' he drawled, his voice infuriatingly calm as she sat beside him, gritting her teeth with frustration at her predicament.

'You seemed delighted at the thought of a lift, until you suddenly and quite inexplicably changed your mind,' he added, bringing the car down to a more reasonable speed. 'So, why are you so anxious to get to Shrewsbury?'

'It's none of your damn business,' she snapped nervously.

'Tsk, tsk!' he murmured. 'I should watch that temper of yours, Alicia. Otherwise you're going to be a shrewish old harridan by the time you're thirty!'

'Thank you!' she glared at his arrogant profile. Mr Pemberton was absolutely right, she thought as she turned her head to stare out of the window, trying to calm down and ignore the amused, taunting voice of the man sitting beside her. She felt ridiculously guilty about her deceitful behaviour—which was crazy, since it wasn't *her* fault that he'd practically kidnapped her just now. There was no doubt that it was going to be much better to let the professionals sort out the dispute between Giles and herself. They seemed to strike sparks off each other every time they met, and not only did he have the ability to make her lose her temper in five seconds flat, but he appeared to take considerable pleasure in doing so. Dealing with this hard, tough man was practically impossible at the best of times. Goodness knew what he'd be like— face to face—if he knew that she was planning to fight him over the farm! It had been one thing to enjoy the thought of his fury on discovering her intentions, but, quite frankly, she didn't want to be anywhere near him when he heard of what she was planning to do. Definitely *a very bad scene*, as Polly would say.

Giles gave a heavy sigh. 'I do wish I knew what was going through that beautiful head of yours. Ever since you returned to the village, I've done my best to help you. But it certainly hasn't been easy!' He gave a harsh laugh.

'Help? What help?' she retorted quickly.

'Well . . . I don't doubt your ability to run Winterfloods, but without a stockman you've obviously been in some difficulty. Which is why I came down to help get the sheep into the barn, and also why I sent Mr Bates along to oversee the lambing. God knows, I'm not asking for your gratitude, Alicia, but do you *really* have to fight me every inch of the way?' he ground out in exasperation, taking a hand off the wheel and pushing it roughly through his thick, dark hair.

'I—I am grateful for your help,' she said stiffly. 'And for the help of old Tom Bates. I—er—I know I should have thanked you for sending him down to the farm, but this is the first time I've seen you since he arrived. And . . . and if you hadn't kidnapped me so suddenly just now—well, I'd have remembered to say thank you, wouldn't I?'

Giles swore briefly under his breath. 'I've already said that I didn't want your gratitude, and you don't have to justify your actions . . .'

'I'm not!' she quickly snapped back, knowing full well that she was doing just that. Even if she hadn't wanted to see him, Alicia realised that she should at least have telephoned to thank him for his help. And if he hadn't served that damned eviction notice, she almost certainly would have done so . . .

'Wake up, Alicia!'

'What . . .?'

Giles sighed. 'I was asking where you'd like me to drop you off? If you can bring yourself to talk to me, that is,' he added with hard irony.

'Yes . . . I'm sorry . . . St John's Hill, please.'

'Very well. And now, if you'll forgive me for the temerity in asking such a question—how are you intending to return to Eastdale?'

Oh, lord—she hadn't thought about the necessity to plan her return journey. What on earth was she going to do? she asked herself as he brought the car to a halt.

'You haven't given it a thought, have you?' he said drily, accurately reading her mind. 'I'll be returning about mid-afternoon, so I suggest that you leave a message for me at the Prince Rupert hotel, saying where you want to be picked up. Okay?'

'Yes . . . um . . . thank you,' she mumbled, struggling to undo her seat belt.

'For God's sake, stop thanking me!' His mouth twisted wryly as he shifted in his seat and turned to face her; the silence in the car was almost deafening. 'We once had a relationship that, for me, was very important,' he said at last. 'I know it's been a long time, and a great deal of water has passed under the bridge——' he hesitated, taking hold of one of her hands. 'But can't we at least try to start again, Alicia?' he asked gently.

Staring up at the sensual curve of his lips and the glowing warmth in his grey eyes. Alicia could feel herself softening, her senses assailed by the force of his strong, physical attraction which seemed almost overwhelming within the close confines of the low sports car. Almost—but not quite. This is the man who two-timed you eight years ago—and with that eviction notice he's planning to do it again! she reminded herself, frantically trying to ignore the sick excitement which shivered down her backbone as he slowly drew her towards him.

'Surely there's no reason why we can't be friends?' he murmured softly, his breath fanning her cheek. 'There's no need for us to be continually fighting one another, hmm . . .?'

'Since . . . since *you* started this particular fight—yes, there is!' she retorted breathlessly, forcing herself to tear her hand away from his grasp, and scrambling quickly from the car before he realised what was happening.

'For God's sake . . .!' Giles swore violently under his breath.

'I don't want to be at loggerheads with you,' she

told the angry face glaring at her from within the Porsche. 'But it *is* you who's drawn up the battle lines, not me. Goodbye,' she added curtly, slamming the door shut and stepping back on to the pavement.

Waiting as he furiously slammed the car into gear and roared away down the street, Alicia felt her legs to be distinctly wobbly as she made her way towards a large Georgian town house, which displayed a shiny brass plate saying, 'Truscott & Co.'. With grand offices like this to support, it was obvious that any advice she was given was going to cost her a small fortune, she thought wryly as she walked up the steps. However, she was still feeling disturbed and upset by that scene in the car, and she knew that she simply wasn't capable of dealing with Giles on her own. If this Mr Truscott could get that two-timing rat out of her hair, his advice would be cheap at any price!

Edmund Truscott was a surprise, Alicia thought, as he smiled and offered her a cup of coffee. She had expected that he would be a contemporary of Mr Pemberton, instead of which he was a tall, slim, dark-haired man who couldn't be more than thirty-eight, at the most. He was really very attractive, she decided, watching as he settled back in his chair and looked at the notes he had been taking.

'Now, Lady Preston. You've outlined your problem, and I've also noted that you have decided to make a firm and serious application for the tenancy of Winterfloods Farm. So what I have to do now is to explain the conditions which you must satisfy if your claim is to be successful. There are three main items: firstly, you must have had experience of farming on the land in question.' He gave her a warm smile. 'We would have no trouble in fulfilling that requirement, since I see that you were actively engaged in farmwork up until eight years ago. Secondly, you must have adequate capital at your disposal to stock and run the farm.'

'What sort of sum would be regarded as "adequate"?' she asked.

'For a five-hundred-acre farm . . .?' He looked at the ceiling for a moment, and then named a sum.

Alicia smiled and gave a brief shrug. 'That would present no problem, and I can give you the address of my bankers if you should need confirmation of that fact.'

'Fine.' He beamed back at her. 'The third item is that you, Lady Preston, must have no other job. I take it that you have no other occupation or profession . . .?'

'Well, other than being a widow and a stepmother—no, I haven't.'

'Very well.' He gave her another of his warm, engaging smiles. 'It seems to me that you appear to have a very reasonable case, and I suggest that you allow me to contact Smith, Garratt and Robinson, making a formal claim to Winterfloods Farm on your behalf.'

'There is just one point on which I'd like some advice.' She paused to marshal her thoughts. 'I can't think of any particular reason at the moment, but if the arbitration went my way, could I still give up the tenancy to Mr Ratcliffe if at any time I wanted to do so? I must add,' she assured him, 'that it's extremely unlikely, but it has occurred to me that I might become seriously ill, for instance, and therefore couldn't continue to farm. I also haven't had the opportunity to discuss this matter with my stepdaughter, although I'm quite sure she will be delighted at my decision.'

Mr Truscott nodded his head. 'That's a very good point. If you gained the tenancy, and I think you have an excellent chance of doing so, you would find yourself in a remarkably strong position. By serving the notice to quit, Mr Ratcliffe has made it clear that he definitely wants your farm. Therefore, if you should decide to give it up at a future date, for whatever reason, then Mr Ratcliffe would undoubtedly have to pay you a large sum of money in return.'

Alicia's eyes widened. 'Even if I offered to give up the farm only a few months after gaining the tenancy? Why on earth should he do that?'

'Once you have been granted the farm, Mr Ratcliffe has effectively lost it—and any profit from the land, other than rent—for the rest of your lifetime. And possibly for at least another generation, if you should marry and have a son to follow you. Now, as you are only twenty-four,' he smiled, 'you can see that Mr Ratcliffe would have to wait a *very* long time before he could get his hands on the farm. Oh, yes, he'd pay a considerable sum for the tenancy, there's no doubt about that!'

'Really?'

He leaned back in his chair. 'If you found yourself in such a position, I certainly wouldn't advise you to take anything less than a hundred thousand pounds, and we could very possibly settle for double that amount.'

'Goodness!' Alica looked at him in astonishment for a moment, and then suddenly found herself laughing almost hysterically. 'Oh, dear, I'm sorry,' she said, wiping the tears of laughter from her eyes. 'I couldn't help thinking of the expression on Giles Ratcliffe's face when he hears the news! I know, it's dreadful and I ought to be thoroughly ashamed of myself.' She gave Edmund Truscott a guilty smile. 'But really, you know, it's the perfect squelch! If Giles hadn't behaved so badly by giving me only three weeks' notice to leave the farm, I'd have quietly left of my own accord. Instead of which, he's prodded me into taking this action. If I win the tenancy—even if I subsequently decide to give it up—Mr Giles Ratcliffe is going to find himself well and truly over a barrel. Right?'

'Er . . . quite right,' Mr Truscott agreed.

Alicia sighed. 'The whole business is quite crazy,

isn't it? Still, I don't see that Giles has given me any choice in the matter. Very well. You'd better get in touch with Mr Ratcliffe's agents, and set the ball rolling.'

'It will be a most interesting case, and there are one or two points about which I'd like a little more clarification,' he said, glancing down at his watch. 'Unfortunately, it seems that time has flown by. I wonder if you are free to have lunch with me—and we could then discuss the remaining items in a more relaxed atmosphere?'

'Yes, I—I think I can manage that,' Alicia agreed.

'Splendid!' He beamed at the girl sitting in front of his desk. She was, without doubt, quite the most beautiful woman he'd ever seen in his life. 'I'll just call and make a reservation at the Prince Rupert hotel in Butcher Row, and then we'll be off.'

'Are you sure I can't persuade you to try anything? I can thoroughly recommend the crème brulée, for instance.'

Alicia smiled at Edmund Truscott, but continued to shake her head at the waitress standing beside her. 'After that delicious home-made soup and the roast lamb, I'm afraid I really couldn't eat another thing. Just coffee, please.'

Edmund gazed at the lovely woman sitting beside him, dressed rather severely in a slim black dress, over which she wore a long double row of superb pearls, her beautifully shaped head with its classical profile enhanced by the smooth, silky sweep of her ash-blonde hair caught into a chignon at the base of her neck. Knowing that he was not an over-imaginative man, he was surprised to find himself thinking, as he watched Alicia surveying the other customers in the restaurant with her wide, brilliant blue eyes, that if Helen of Troy had possessed half of this woman's beauty, he could at last understand the motivation behind the Trojan wars.

Leaning back in her seat, and quite oblivious of Edmund's concentrated gaze, Alicia glanced around the room and tried to remember when she had last been to lunch in this ancient, fifteenth-century hotel. It must have been with her father, she decided, recalling how she used to be so excited as a small girl, when he would not only take her into Shrewsbury on Market Day, but they would have a slap, bang-up lunch at the Prince Rupert before going home. Not that he and she had lunched here, in this rather grand Cavalier Restaurant, but in one of the smaller of the three other dining-rooms in the large hotel. How grown-up and sophisticated she had felt, being allowed to order a meal for herself, and to know that she had her father's undivided attention. Always so busy on the farm, John Howard hadn't been able to give much time to his daughter, but those occasional outings together had been precious ones which she had always treasured. No wonder she had been so shattered when he died, and no wonder that her mother had sometimes despaired of being able to control her wayward daughter, who had grown wild and rebellious without her father's firm hand. Was that the real reason why her mother had married Jed? To provide a father for her daughter? Alicia frowned as she realised that she'd never considered that aspect of her mother's remarriage before. Too selfishly absorbed by her own unhappiness at the time, she had also been far too young to understand the reasons behind her mother's decision.

The arrival of a waitress with their coffee brought Alicia back to the present, and to the fact that she had been so caught up in the past that she hadn't been listening to a word Edmund had been saying.

'. . . also claim that as a woman, Lady Preston, you would not be capable of running a farm on your own.'

'What absolute nonsense!' Alicia retorted crisply.

'Who, in this day and age, would be so foolish as to make a ridiculous claim like that?'

'Well . . .' Edmund shrugged. 'I think that you must be prepared for the fact that Mr Ratcliffe may try to argue that point.'

'He would—the sexist, male chauvinist pig!'

The land agent gave her a nervous smile. 'Whatever your feelings about Mr Ratcliffe, I must urge you not to give vent to them at the tenancy hearing. Especially since the arbitration panel is likely to be composed of men.'

Alicia laughed. 'No, I can see that would be a grave mistake! Don't worry, I promise to be as sweet as honey towards Giles at the hearing—although I can't guarantee to hold my tongue afterwards!'

'I can assure you, Lady Preston, that I . . .'

'I do think we know each other well enough by now for you to call me by my Christian name, don't you, Edmund?' she smiled.

'Yes . . . indeed.' His cheeks flushed slightly. 'As I was about to say—er—Alicia, we seem to have covered the main points of your case, and I really don't think you have anything to worry about.'

'One small matter that did occur to me . . .' Alicia's voice faltered, her words dying away as she saw Giles' tall, broad-shouldered figure entering the restaurant. A moment later, having cast a swift glance around the room, he began to move in the direction of their table.

'Oh, lord!' she muttered under her breath, before looking up at his approach with a face from which she quickly tried to erase all expression.

'Ah, Edmund, how nice to see you again,' Giles said smoothly, as the land agent rose to his feet and they shook hands. 'I didn't know you knew Lady Preston?'

There was a definite question mark in his voice, the narrowed grey eyes searching Alicia's face which paled beneath his intense gaze. She could feel her skin grow cold as she absorbed his hard, daunting presence, and was dismayed to find herself cowardly wishing that she didn't have to fight this formidable man.

'Ah, yes,' Edmund replied blandly. 'Lady Preston has been consulting me about Winterfloods Farm.'

'Why?'

Alicia stiffened at Giles' terse demand. *Oh, heavens!* she thought, suddenly feeling sick with apprehension. Edmund can't be going to tell Giles everything? *Not right here and now?*

CHAPTER SEVEN

HOLDING her breath, Alicia braced herself to face the fiery explosion which would inevitably follow when Giles learnt about her plans for the farm. It soon became apparent, however, that she had no need to be so apprehensive, Edmund Truscott swiftly demonstrating that he was perfectly capable of dealing with Giles Ratcliffe.

'As far as Winterfloods Farm is concerned, there have been various aspects under discussion,' he said in a calm, mild voice, apparently unperturbed by Giles' sharp question. 'Although we haven't yet talked about the future of the animals on the farm, have we, Alicia?'

'No—no, we haven't,' she murmured, almost sagging with relief at the adroit way Edmund had avoided telling an outright lie.

Giles' mouth tightened, his grey eyes growing hard and stormy as he registered the warmth in the reassuring smile Edmund Truscott gave Alicia, before he was distracted by a voice hailing him across the room.

'Giles—darling! Where on earth have you been? I've been looking for you simply everywhere!'

It didn't take Alicia more than a second or two to note that the woman moving swiftly across the floor towards them was quite outstandingly good-looking. As she clutched Giles' arm, reaching up on tip-toe to plant a kiss on his cheek, before turning to give them all a dazzling smile, Alicia knew with absolute

122

certainty who she was, even before Giles performed the introductions.

'Melanie, you know Edmund, of course. But I don't think you've met Lady Preston,' he said blandly. 'Alicia, this is Melanie Todd, who has recently bought a house in the village; but perhaps you already know that?' he added with a sardonic smile.

'Hello, Edmund. How are you, darling?' Melanie gave the land agent a peck on the cheek, before slowly turning around to view Alicia with unconcealed interest.

Now that she could see her more clearly, Alicia realised that Melanie wasn't quite as young as she had at first seemed. Possibly about twenty-nine or thirty, but clearly fighting the years all the way, there was no doubt that she was sensationally attractive. Dark, almost black hair rippled down to her shoulders, and the dark eyes blinking at the sight of Alicia were fringed with long, thick eyelashes casting faint shadows on her clear olive skin. The cream wool dress she was wearing was classically simple, and might have been designed to emphasise her distinct sensuality, clinging to her rounded breasts and slim hips, and providing a strong impression of deliberately flaunted, sexual provocation. Suddenly feeling unaccountably weary and depressed, Alicia hadn't the shred of a doubt that Melanie Todd and Giles were currently enjoying— to use one of Polly's slang phrases—an 'in-bed relationship'.

Her attention was distracted from the vision standing in front of her, as Giles put his hand on Edmund's shoulder. 'If I could just have a quiet word with you, about the arrangements for next week's NFU meeting? I won't be a minute, Melanie,' he added as he drew Edmund aside.

'This always happens when I haven't had any breakfast, and I'm hungry enough to eat a horse,' Melanie groaned as she came over to sit down beside

Alicia. 'It's been hell in my shop this morning, too. Men are the living end, aren't they?'

'I . . .'

'I know what you're going to say,' the dark girl sighed dramatically. 'We can't do without them, right?'

'Well, I . . .'

'I knew you'd agree with me! A necessary evil, I call them,' she gave a wry laugh. 'I mean, I was absolutely fed up with my rich, old, incredibly boring ex-husband, but when he went off to live with his ugly secretary—honestly, darling, she wasn't a day under forty-five!—I found I really missed having the ghastly old stick around the house! After all, a girl does need to have someone to pour her a drink and chat to over dinner, don't you agree?'

All the time she was talking, Alicia had been aware of Melanie's dark eyes flicking over her clothes, assessing to the last penny exactly how much the black woollen dress and the pearls had cost. Much good may it do her, Alicia thought drily. Especially as I normally wear jeans and rubber boots!

'How long have you been living in the village?' she asked, when she could get a word in edgeways.

'Well, it seems like ages, of course, but in fact I only moved into my cottage a year ago. You can't live in Eastdale, though, because I'm certain that I haven't seen you before . . . *Oh!*' she gave a childish, high-pitched squeak. 'Silly me! Of course I know who you are! You must be Jed Black's stepdaughter. I've heard all about you from Mrs Jenkins—frightful old witch, isn't she?'

'Frightful,' Alicia agreed, realising that she mustn't make the mistake of thinking that Melanie was stupid. She might sound like the dark equivalent of a dumb blonde, but there was a chilly, intelligent gleam in those black eyes that made the woman's 'poor-little-me' act extremely unconvincing.

'I do think that it's about time someone formed a

"Down With Mrs Jenkins" society, don't you?'
Melanie was saying. 'I'd been warned about her when
I first came to live in the village, of course, so I
steamed into her shop and gave a really startling
performance of myself in the role of the local tart!'
She giggled. 'Poor Mrs Jenkins, I thought she'd die
of apoplexy! Quite honestly, I haven't had such fun
for ages!'

'Yes, I—er—I rather gathered that you were very
convincing in the role,' Alicia murmured drily.

'Oh, yes, as far as she's concerned, I'm destined
for the hell fires of damnation,' Melanie agreed, only
a quick flash in her eyes betraying the fact
that Alicia's last remark had scored a direct hit.
'Incidentally, the evil old bag told me all about you,
too.'

'Oh, really?'

Melanie's eyes sparked with malice. 'I bet you're
dying to know *all*, aren't you?'

'No, I'm not,' Alicia said firmly, realising with a
sinking heart that she might as well have saved her
breath.

'According to Mrs-news-of-the-world-Jenkins, Lady
Preston—she really goes for your title!—was the poor
but lovely Cinderella of the village, leaving her glass
slipper and the local prince behind when she ran off
to London. There she apparently captured yet another
prince or, more accurately, an ancient knight of the
realm, and has now returned to the village in triumph
as a beautiful, rich widow with a stepdaughter in
tow!'

'What absolute rubbish—the woman's a menace!'
Alicia muttered angrily.

'Well, it could be a lot worse. In fact, rather
surprisingly, it seems as if Mrs Jenkins approves of
you. And that must be an all-time record—don't you
think?' Melanie put her dark head on one side and
coolly regarded Alicia. 'I hear that Mrs J is holding
you up as a shining example of just how—if she

really tries *very* hard—, a girl can get on in the
world!'

'Oh, yes?' Alicia tried to sound bored, although
she was simmering with rage and well aware that
under the guise of her artless conversation, Melanie
Todd was being poisonously bitchy. That was another
item to add to her list of grievances against Giles, she
thought bitterly, glancing over to where the two men
were still talking together. How dared he dump his
current mistress down at her table like this? She was
supposed to be having a quiet lunch with Edmund,
and she needed Melanie's verbal sword thrusts like a
dog needed fleas!

'They say women gossip, but this is ridiculous!'
Melanie said, her eyes following Alicia's. 'However,
I'm glad to have the opportunity to have a brief,
private word.' She lowered her voice. 'I gather that
you and Giles used to be very—er—close at one
time . . .?'

'Were we really? How interesting. Why don't you
tell me about it?' Alicia said coolly, drawing on her
experience of life in the bitchy jet stream of London
society as she forced herself to gaze serenely back at
the woman who was regarding her so intently.

'Ah . . . I think I'd better rephrase that question!'
Melanie was clearly not a whit abashed at having
been put firmly in her place. Alicia could now readily
understand why this woman, with such dazzling good
looks and a hide like a rhinoceros, should have had
Mrs Jenkins practically climbing the wall. She
was virtually unsnubbable—not to say, completely
unstoppable!

'What I *meant* to say—or rather to ask you—
concerns the present rather than the past,' Melanie
continued, her dark eyes flicking briefly towards Giles'
tall figure. 'You see, I'm a great one for putting my
cards on the table . . .'

I'll just bet you are! Alicia thought grimly.

'. . . and of course, I'm absolutely crazy about

Giles. So, naturally, I'm dying to know if you're still keen on him. A girl does like to know where the competition is coming from, if you see what I mean?'

Alicia gave a snort of derisory laughter. 'As far as Giles is concerned, there's no need to look in my direction. Quite honestly, you are more than welcome to the wretched man. There's no question of having to worry about any competition from me—far from it!'

'Oh, great!'

'I wouldn't get too excited, if I were you,' Alicia said bluntly, rising from the table as she saw that the men had at last finished talking. 'Any woman tangling with Giles Ratcliffe definitely needs to have her head examined. However, if you're happy to take your place in the queue—alongside all his other girl-friends—well . . .' she gave a careless shrug of her shoulders, delighted to see that Melanie was looking somewhat shaken by her words, 'then all I can say, Mrs Todd, is that I wish you the very best of British luck!'

Alicia reached forward to switch on the radio, humming along with the music as the strains of a popular song filled the car. Why on earth hadn't she thought of buying herself a decent vehicle before now? Glancing around the spacious interior of the brand new Range Rover, she smiled happily at the thought of no longer having to wrestle with Jed's ancient old vehicle, not to mention the sheer, blissful relief of knowing that she wasn't likely to break down every time she ventured out on to the road!

She had, in fact, been contemplating the purchase of a reliable car when she had been sitting in Edmund Truscott's office. After all, now she was intending to stay on at the farm, she was going to need some transport on which she could depend. But it wasn't until after lunch in the hotel, when Giles had been so aggressive, that she had translated the vague idea into immediate action.

Edmund had been very apologetic at having deserted her while he talked to Giles. 'I'm so sorry, Alicia,' he had said, hurrying over to join her as she rose from the table. 'Perhaps you will allow me to make amends for my behaviour, and let me take you out to dinner tomorrow night?'

Knowing that without Polly's help this weekend she was likely to be busy on the farm, she was just about to refuse when she realised that Giles was standing beside her, and had clearly been listening to every word. It was also clear from his rigid stance and the angry glitter in his grey eyes that he violently disapproved of her going out with Edmund.

Where or with whom I have dinner has nothing to do with him, she thought angrily, her fury increasing as Melanie came over to join them, leaning her voluptuous figure against Giles and staring adoringly up into his face. Here he was, boldly flaunting his current mistress, when only a few hours earlier he had been busy chatting *her* up in the Porsche—'Can't we be friends?', indeed!

'I'd *love* to join you for dinner.' She gave Edmund a wide, brilliant smile. 'Why don't you telephone me tomorrow, hmm?' she added in a low, husky voice.

From the slight flush on Edmund's cheeks, she knew that she had succeeded in her aim of sounding ripe with sexual promise, and that the main target of her performance, Giles himself, was visibly trembling with rage. Good! Why shouldn't he have a dose of his own medicine? Standing there with that . . . that woman draped all over him, he had absolutely no right to be acting like a dog in the manger—and for two pins, she'd tell him so!

She had her wish rather sooner than she expected. 'Excuse me,' Giles said to the others as he grasped her arm and drew her roughly aside. 'What in hell do you think you're playing at?' he grated in a low, ominous voice. 'I won't have . . .'

'You won't have what?' she snapped angrily back at him under her breath. 'Isn't one woman enough for you? I'd have thought you'd have your hands full coping with Melanie—there's certainly a lot of her to get hold of!' She gave a snort of grim laughter. 'Besides, you're being ridiculous. The way you're acting, anyone would think you were jealous of Edmund, for heaven's sake!'

'Of course I am, you stupid girl!' he rasped, staring grimly down at her, before the anger seemed to drain away from his rigid figure and he gave her a sardonic grin. 'I'm just as jealous of Edmund as you are of Melanie—so why don't we stop all this nonsense? I'll collect you from the hotel here, at three o'clock, and . . .'

'Oh, no, you won't. I—I've made other plans,' she said quickly, suddenly making a firm decision to buy herself a car. She was *definitely* not going to be trapped in that Porsche of his again—and if she couldn't find anything to buy, well . . . she could always hire a taxi, couldn't she?

Luckily, she had found just what she wanted at practically the first garage she visited, and now here she was, the proud possessor of a brand new Range Rover. It had been a splendid idea to buy herself some transport, and one that was made even better by the sight of Giles' fury when she'd refused his offer of a lift.

Nearly home now, she told herself as she spun the vehicle off the main road and on down the small lane to Winterfloods. Home . . . It was a small word, but in the context of her past life, it meant a great deal. She really had 'come home' at last, and despite all her problems she felt a small, quiet glow of happiness as she drew up in the farmyard.

As soon as she opened the back door, she realised that something was dreadfully wrong. It was the

strong, almost suffocating smell of sulphur that she
noticed first of all. And then when her eyes had
grown accustomed to the ill-lit interior of the back
scullery, she realised that the walls were heavily
coated with soot, and she was standing in warm dirty
water which contained lumps of coke and cinders.
Oh, my God! she thought. *The boiler must have
burst!*

Stepping gingerly across the filthy floor, Alicia
followed the trail of water into the kitchen, which
was in the same disgusting condition as the scullery.
The large, oil-fired Aga stove, used solely for cooking,
seemed to be still alight, and that was the only bright
spark in a thoroughly dismal situation. She must get
to the phone and call a plumber immediately, although
she realised that her chances of getting anyone at
four-thirty on a Friday afternoon were very slim
indeed. She was just thumbing her way through the
Yellow Pages, when the phone rang. Lifting the
receiver, she heard Elsie's voice.

'Yes . . . yes . . . I'm glad you're feeling better,'
she said, cutting in on the old housekeeper's long
description of her illness. 'I'm sorry if I sound
unsympathetic,' she added, 'but I've just come home
to find an incredible mess. It looks as if the old boiler
has burst, although I haven't investigated the rest of
the house yet. You don't know a good plumber, do
you?'

'Oh, my lord. I just knew that dang old boiler
would be a-going one of these days. The times what I
told Jed . . .'

'Elsie . . .!' Alicia groaned. 'We both know all
about Jed's meanness—but that isn't going to mend
the boiler, is it? Can you think of anyone who can
help me? I've got to try and stop the water somehow,
and I can't even remember the whereabouts of the
stopcock.'

'That there stopcock, what turns off the rising
main, is under the sink. You can't miss it—it's at the

back on the left-hand side,' Elsie said quickly. 'Now, you be off to see to that, and I'll put on my thinking cap, and see if I can't find a man what'll help you.'

Having managed to screw shut the heavy metal handle, Alicia left the kitchen and walked down the corridor towards the main rooms of the house. She was dismayed to find that the soot and sulphurous smoke had covered everything with a fine layer of greasy dust, although as she mounted the stairs, she could see that it didn't seem to have affected the upper landing. Unfortunately, the bathroom and some of the bedrooms told a different story. The pipes in the bathroom, and those running to the basins in the bedrooms, had clearly sprung various leaks, and there were puddles everywhere—and they seemed to be growing larger every minute.

She was in her bedroom, trying to mop up some of the water with a pile of towels, when she heard a shout from downstairs. 'I'm up here,' she called out as she tried to staunch the flow of water. 'Oh, it's hopeless!' she groaned, sitting back on her heels and contemplating the soaking wet towels.

'I must agree, it doesn't look too good,' Giles' voice said from behind her.

'Oh, lord. What on earth are you doing here?' She brushed a weary hand through her hair. 'I was hoping you were a plumber.'

'No, I'm afraid not,' he said, coming forward and taking her arm to help her to her feet. 'However, I have called out a man who lives in one of my houses in the village. He should be here any minute now,' he added, glancing down at his watch.

'Giles Ratcliffe to my rescue again!' She gave a short, harsh laugh, before she realised that she did need his help, and whatever the disagreements between them, the very least she could do was to be duly grateful. 'Oh, I'm sorry,' she said with a tired smile. 'I don't really know what's happened . . .'

'I should think that it's the thaw, don't you? I

expect your pipes were frozen, and they burst when the temperature suddenly became warmer.' He led her over to sit down on the bed. 'Now why don't you pack a few things, while I go and look over the damage. I'll be back in a minute,' he added over his shoulder as he left the room.

Pack . . .? What on earth was he talking about? Alicia shook her head in bewilderment, before she quickly stripped off her black dress and hurriedly changed into a pair of jeans. She was just pulling on a sweater when Giles returned.

'The plumber's downstairs,' he said. 'Apparently you've already done the most important thing, which is to turn off the stopcock. He's busy draining the tank in the roof, but there isn't anything more he can do until tomorrow.' He looked around the room. 'I thought you'd have some things packed by now?'

Alicia sighed. 'I don't know what you're talking about.'

'You can't possibly be thinking of staying here tonight? This place is far too filthy, and without any heat you'll freeze. The temperature is falling again, and as soon as we go the plumber is switching off the electricity. It's too dangerous with all that water about,' he explained patiently. 'So . . . pack what you need for tonight, because you'll be staying up at the Hall.'

'Oh, no!' she retorted quickly. 'I—I can go to a hotel, or . . .'

'God give me strength!' he groaned. 'I'm merely offering you a bed for the night. And no—I don't mean *my* bed, you stupid woman!' he added, accurately reading the expression on her face. 'There are lots of guest rooms at the Hall, and if you can't see that you'll be far more comfortable there—you must be a complete idiot! Besides, what hotel is going to take you, looking like that?' he said cruelly, dragging her over towards a large mirror.

Furious at being talked to as if she really were an

idiot, Alicia flinched as she saw the black smuts on her face, and the long greasy streaks of oil on her hair where she'd brushed it off her face with her filthy hands. Even if she went to a hotel, she'd first of all have to find somewhere to wash both herself and her hair, she thought helplessly.

'Now, I don't want any more nonsense,' Giles said sternly. 'I give you my word of honour that you will merely be staying as a guest in my house—nothing more, okay?'

'But—but I haven't seen to the cows, or . . .'

Giles refused to listen to any more of her arguments, insisting that he and Tom Bates would see to the animals. He was giving her only ten minutes to do her packing before the electricity was turned off, and would she please pull her finger out and get on with it?

Any further protests seemed to be a waste of time, and it wasn't long before she had thanked the plumber and was in Giles' Range Rover, on her way to Eastdale Hall. Everything had happened so quickly that she still felt quite numb. The pain of seeing the old house in such a state had been traumatic, and the plumber had only shaken his head with gloom when she'd asked him if the ceilings of the downstairs rooms were going to be all right.

The sound of wheels on gravel jerked her from her self-absorption, and she looked up to see that they had arrived at the Hall. 'I could easily have driven up here in my own car,' she protested, 'and I still don't think . . .'

'Forget it, Alicia!' Giles' hard voice cut across her objections as they came to a halt outside the ornate porch of the Jacobean mansion. 'We've already discussed the matter—*ad nauseam*—and although I know you would never have come to my house of your own volition, we also both know that you haven't any real alternative,' he said, undoing his seat belt. 'Okay, so I may have grabbed this opportunity, but . . .'

'"Grab" is the right word!' Alicia glared at him. 'If you think that I'm going to join the list of all your other women, being chased round the bedroom . . .' her heated protest was interrupted by his dry, mocking laughter.

'I find your belief in my sexual ability—not to say stamina!—deeply flattering. However, my dear Alicia, I have no intention, at the moment, anyway, of putting my lascivious hands on your lily-white body. I'll repeat my promise: while you are a guest in my house, your person will be inviolate—sacred—untouchable, etc, etc! On top of which, if you're really so worried about my bestial appetite,' he added sardonically, 'I hope you will accept the chaperonage of my housekeeper, Mrs Renshaw, who has been looking forward to seeing you once again.'

'Elsie's sister?' she asked, temporarily diverted from her annoyance at being shanghaied by Giles. 'What's she doing here? I thought she and her husband worked for Sir Joshua Masters at Fairlee Priory?'

'They came to look after me six years ago, when old Sir Joshua died, and I can't think how I ever managed without them. Here's Renshaw now,' said Giles as the upright, grey-haired butler came down the steps towards them. 'I should hate to upset him, so could you please save your cries about "rape and pillage", until we get inside?'

'Your sense of humour is absolutely pathetic!' she hissed, before opening her door. 'Hello, Renshaw. How very nice to see you again,' she said, smiling at the man she had known since her childhood.

'It's a pleasure to see you, too, Lady Preston,' he said gravely. 'Mrs Renshaw has been busy getting your room ready, and we both hope you will be very comfortable here at the Hall.'

'I'm sure I shall,' she assured him, following as he led the way up the steps, and into the large panelled hall. 'You seemed to have been damned confident that I'd come here . . .' she whispered accusingly to Giles, who merely shrugged and indicated that she should follow Renshaw up the long flight of stairs.

'That was a marvellous meal, Mrs Renshaw. I haven't eaten so well for ages!' Alicia looked around the large, well-appointed kitchen, so much larger than that at Winterfloods. She had forgotten just how large the Hall was, and although houses remembered from one's childhood were supposed to look much smaller when visited years later, Eastdale Hall was still an enormous mansion by anyone's standards.

'Well, Miss Alicia, I must say, it's a fair treat to see you again.' Elsie and her sister could easily be taken for twins, thought Alicia, smiling at the round, squat figure of Giles' housekeeper. It might be Elsie's dark little boot-button eyes regarding her so closely. 'I hope your room was to your satisfaction?' the older woman continued. 'You just let me know if you is needing anything.'

'I'm sure I won't. However, I must thank you for getting everything ready for me in such a short space of time.' There was no doubt that Mrs Renshaw had thought of just about everything. The blue and white chintz curtains, which matched the design on the wallpaper, had been drawn and the bedside lamps lit to give the large bedroom a warm, cosy glow. The adjoining private bathroom had provided lots of hot water, and Alicia had lain there for some time soaking off the grime from the farm, although she had been forced to wash her hair three times before she felt confident she had removed all the dust and dirt.

'What's going to happen about that there farmhouse of yours? Can the plumber make it all good again?' Mrs Renshaw asked.

Alicia shrugged. 'Goodness knows. Everything is in such a mess. It might be a good idea to pull out all the old plumbing and start again with a brand new system. I'll have to see tomorrow.'

'We all knows as how that dang ol' Jed never did nothing to the house. Well, m'dear,' the older woman beamed at her, 'you knows full well we'll be real pleased if you stays here while the work is going on. Elsie said you was looking a bit peaky.'

Alicia laughed. 'Peaky? Another meal like the one I've just had, and I won't be able to get into my clothes! And although it's kind of you to say so, I'm afraid that I can't possibly stay here for more than one night,' she added firmly.

Contrary to all her grave misgivings, Giles had behaved perfectly when she had come downstairs for dinner. Merely contenting himself with a murmured, 'You look charming,' as his eyes had swept over her midnight blue silk dress, he had confined his conversation to innocuous topics. In fact, to her great surprise, she had enjoyed the evening so far—not least for Mrs Renshaw's superb cooking!

'That veal was truly superb,' she said. 'Although I really came in to say that I've been trying to teach myself to cook, and will you show me how to make those chocolate profiteroles?'

'What you wants to learn cooking for, I don't know. Still, I'll be pleased to show you how I does that dish. Elsie said as how we had to feed you up real well.'

'Come on, Mrs Renshaw, you know Elsie! She'd have me the size of a barrel, if she had her way. However, she's really not at all well at the moment, and I'm a bit worried about her.' She looked at the housekeeper with concern. 'Do you know if she's had the doctor in yet?'

'Yes. I phones her every night, and I told her to stop fiddlin' about, seeing as she's got to look after Fred, as well as you and your young stepdaughter. And she ain't goin' to do that flat on her back, now is she? Still, there's no need to worry, I reckon as she's on the mend, all right.'

'I'm so glad. The farm doesn't seem the same place without her.'

'Well, m'dear, I don't reckon you looks too bad at all. That Elsie, she was always one for worrying. Still an' all, we's right glad you've come back at last,' Mrs Renshaw added, resting her flour-covered hands on her hips. 'Poor Mr Ratcliffe, he's had a rare old time of it, what with his wife and those fancy men of hers. Disgusting she was—an' no mistake! It's time he got married again. We all wants to see him nicely settled down with a new wife, and that's a fact.'

Alicia shrugged. 'Well, I expect he will remarry. Isn't there a Mrs Todd in the offing?' she said carelessly.

'That woman is *not* what we has in mind,' said Mrs Renshaw forcefully. 'A rare flighty piece—and no better than she should be, by all accounts. Right for Mr Ratcliffe, she certainly ain't! Nor fit to run this house, neither,' she added, pushing forward the baking tray. 'Go on, m'dear, you try one of my cheese scones as you always did like. We's going to have them for tea tomorrow.'

'Oh, goodness—I'm so full already! Still . . . mmm, it's delicious,' said Alicia, sinking her teeth into the succulent scone.

'Yes, m'dear,' the housekeeper continued. 'When my sister Elsie tells us as how you is now a widow, and when she says you is coming up for ol' Jed's funeral—well, we hears the call of angels' trumpets, as you might say. It don't take a pair of glasses to see as how you and Mr Ratcliffe was made for each other. A right pigeon pair, and the sooner you both ties the knot, the happier we all will be . . .' She broke off, looking with concern at Alicia who was coughing and spluttering.

'Is you all right, m'dear?'

Alicia gestured helplessly, unable to speak as she

continued to choke on a crumb which had stuck in her throat. 'I . . . can I . . . have a glass of w-water . . .?' she gasped, fighting for breath.

Mrs Renshaw rushed to the sink and came back with a tumbler. 'Here you are, m'dear, you get that down and you'll be all right in a tick.'

'Yes . . . I . . . Oh, goodness, that's better.' Alicia took a deep breath. 'Look, I've got to put the record straight. If you've been saying what I think you've been saying . . .? I must tell you that there's no way I could ever . . . I mean, there's not the slightest possibility of Mr Ratcliffe and me . . .'

'I do hope you're not giving me a bad name, Alicia!' a deep voice drawled behind her back, and she whirled around to see Giles standing in the doorway of the large kitchen.

'Get away, Mr Ratcliffe! That's something she wouldn't ever be a-doing of. And I won't let you be teasing of this lovely girl, neither! Now, I'll thank you both to leave my kitchen. Renshaw will be along with the coffee, directly.'

Beaming at what she obviously thought of as a pair of young lovers, she shooed them from the room. Alicia managed to contain herself as she walked silently beside Giles, and it was only when he closed the door of the drawing-room that she felt able to give vent to her feelings.

'My God! I can't think why I've been so blind. It's the damn village Mafia at work again. Well, I won't have it!' she stormed.

'Why don't you calm down, and tell me what's wrong?' Giles said quietly.

'It's all as plain as day—I can see the whole plot now,' she snarled, hardly aware of his existence as she paced rapidly up and down over the carpet. 'Those two old harpies—on the phone to each other, night and day . . .! They both clearly knew what I was doing, almost before I did myself!'

Giles strode over and caught hold of her arm. 'For

goodness' sake relax!' he said sternly. 'I haven't the slightest idea of what's upsetting you. But I'm sure there's nothing that can't be sorted out, if you'll just sit down and talk about it calmly.'

She looked at him with startled eyes, and then allowed herself to be led over to a wide sofa covered in blue raw silk. 'I'm sorry,' she gestured helplessly. 'I really can't think what's come over me,' she gave a shaky laugh. 'I'm usually quite a cool, collected person—or at least, I always thought I was.' She brushed a distracted hand across her brow.

'Nonsense!' he gave her a wide smile. 'You were always hot-tempered, very emotional, and would fight to the death rather than give in to something you felt was wrong. Which brings me to the point: why all the fuss?'

Alicia took a deep breath, and was just about to tell him about Elsie's and her sister's matchmaking schemes, when she suddenly realised that of course she couldn't. He didn't know anything about it, and telling him would only make her look extremely foolish. He might possibly find it all very amusing, but she doubted it, somehow. Her face burned as she tried to think of some excuse for her fury just now.

'I—er—I was wondering how you came to hear about the burst pipes at the farm, this afternoon? I mean,' she gave him a stiff smile, 'I'm very grateful, of course, even if I wasn't in a good mood when you found me. It's just that it does seem a bit of a coincidence . . . that's all I meant . . .' she said lamely.

'There's nothing very dramatic or extraordinary about it,' he shrugged. 'I returned home, and just as I was about to go and see one of my tenants, Mrs Renshaw asked me to call at Winterfloods. Elsie was apparently worried, after her phone call, as to how you were going to manage in a freezing cold house for the next few days until the boiler was mended.'

Aha! I knew it! Alicia told herself. The two women

had been conspiring together since . . . when? She tried to remember her phone calls to Elsie from London. After Walter died, she had kept in closer touch than before, and it must have been then that the two sisters had got together and hatched their plot. If Giles hadn't been going to Jed's funeral, what was the betting that the Renshaws wouldn't have found an excuse to get him there? And how had he known—spot on—the exact moment when the sheep started lambing . . .? Elsie on the phone again, what else? Alicia tried to see the funny side of the situation, but she could find little to laugh about. It was, in fact, all very embarrassing. Although, thank goodness, it looked as if Giles hadn't a clue what was going on.

'I'm still waiting to hear what's responsible for prompting all that excitement and fury just now.' Giles' smooth drawl broke into her abstracted thoughts.

'Oh—nothing, really,' she muttered, looking up with relief as Renshaw entered the room with a tray. She took the opportunity to move further away along the sofa. It was somehow easier to deal with Giles' strong personality when she wasn't sitting quite so close to him.

He asked her to pour the coffee, and as she lifted the heavy silver pot, Alicia found herself hoping that he was going to tell her—at long last—why he'd served that notice to quit the farm. He would be angry to hear about her counter-proposal, of course, but at least everything would be out in the open, and maybe they could try and discuss the whole business calmly. Despite Mr Pemberton's advice, she was quite prepared to do so if Giles mentioned the subject. The nervous tension resulting from having to keep silent on such an important matter, and feeling so deceitful and guilty at doing so, was making her act in an unusually awkward manner.

'It's been a long time since you ran away from Eastdale.' Giles' voice broke the long silence between them. 'Were you happy with your late husband?' he added quietly, staring down as he stirred his cup of hot coffee.

'What an extraordinary question!' She looked at him in surprise. 'Yes, of course I was. Very happy. Walter was a very dear, kind man, and . . . and I miss him more than I can possibly say.'

'I understand that he left you very well provided for.'

Her hackles rose as she registered the dry, caustic note in his voice. 'I didn't marry Walter for his money, and I would gladly trade every last penny if it would bring him back to me.'

'If you say so.' Giles shrugged, his voice heavy with scepticism.

She flushed indignantly. 'Yes, I damn well do! I had a very happy marriage. I must admit that I've never lacked for the material comforts of life, but money on its own means nothing—not if there isn't kindness and affection as well.'

He gave a snort of derision. 'Is that what you're going to have when you marry someone like Scott Harper—a life of kindness and affection?'

'Me? Marry Scott Harper . . .?' She gazed at him in bewilderment. Scott Harper was an old business colleague of Walter's, and when her husband had died, Scott had asked her to take his place on the board of an organisation the two men had formed some years ago. So, yes, of course she saw Scott every so often, and had attended some charity functions with him—but that was all.

'Where on earth did you get hold of that idea?' she asked.

Giles' mouth tightened. 'I seem to recall having read something in the gossip columns.'

'Oh, come on!' She gave a light, nervous laugh. 'You can't be serious? Nobody takes any notice of that sort of newspaper rubbish. Besides,' she added coldly, 'my private life is none of your business.'

'Very true,' he agreed smoothly, his mocking grey eyes sweeping over her tense figure. 'Except I couldn't help noticing, when you talked about your husband and your happy marriage, that you made no reference to love. It does rather sound as if the emotional temperature in your marriage hardly rose above zero, hmm?'

The sheer audacity of his comment took Alicia's breath away. Humiliatingly aware of the rising tide of crimson covering her cheeks, she clasped her hands tightly together, the knuckles white with tension as she struggled to control her temper.

'You're hardly in a position to criticise, or make snide comments about anyone else's married life, are you?' she said at last, her voice husky with contempt. 'Perhaps I ought to say that I'm sorry you and Camilla didn't manage to make a go of your marriage, but I can't preteɪd that I'm at all surprised. Let's face it, Giles—what you know about the verb "to love" could be written on the back of a postage stamp!'

'And you're the great expert, I suppose?' he retorted grimly.

'In so far as I have known what it is to love someone—yes. That doesn't make me an expert, but at least I know *something* about the emotion. The same can't be said for you! Leaping into bed with any passing female doesn't prove anything, except that you're over-sexed,' she sneered. 'No wonder your marriage to Camilla didn't last more than a year—I'm only amazed that it survived as long as it did!'

His face became a stony mask from which his eyes blazed like chips of grey ice. 'You know nothing about my marriage!' he whispered savagely, grabbing hold of her arm and jerking her violently towards him. Pinned up against his chest, she tried to push him away with her free hand, feeling the strength of the taut muscles beneath her palm, the warmth of his hard body beneath his thin silk shirt and soft cashmere sweater.

'Let go of me!' she stormed.

'I'll let you go—in my own good time!' he snarled. 'You've been the root cause of more unhappiness than I can even begin to describe, so why shouldn't you face hearing the truth, for once? Ever since you've been back, you have made it abundantly clear that you have absolutely no idea about the living hell of my empty marriage.'

'It's nothing to do with me,' she said breathlessly.

'Oh, no? Why else would I have married Camilla? When I lost you to that rich old husband of yours—I neither knew nor cared what I did . . .'

'Don't be ridiculous, Giles!' she retorted sharply, furious at being accused of something which was so patently absurd. 'I had nothing to do with your decision to marry Camilla, and there's no way that I can possibly be blamed for the failure of your marriage. However, you're quite right—I don't want to know about the intimate details of your life with Camilla, thank you very much! Your fiancée told me, eight years ago, that not only did she know all about your little affair with me, but that I was only one among many!' She gave a shrill laugh.

'That's a damn lie!' he thundered. Alicia flinched as she saw his nostrils flare with rage, a dark flush covering his cheeks as he glared at her with incredulity. 'I was *never* engaged to Camilla—not formally, and certainly not before you ran off to London. What's more, I entirely deny your allegations that I'm some sort of local Don Juan . . . quite the reverse, in fact,' he added, his face contorted with bitterness.

'Ha! And what about dear Melanie?' she taunted. 'Don't try and tell me that you haven't been studying her form—because I won't believe you!'

'For God's sake, Alicia!' he groaned. 'Okay—I shouldn't have done it, but surely you can see that I've only been using the girl to try and jerk some response out of you? What Melanie wants and what she gets are two entirely different things. Darling!

You must *know* that I've only ever been interested in you; that what we had between us was very far from being a "little affair"? How could it have been, when I've never ceased thinking about you, wanting you . . .'

She tensed at the thick note in his voice. 'No, Giles . . .' her husky protest was cut short as he suddenly lowered his head, his mouth slowly and softly seducing her lips apart. His hand moved over her body in an intimate caress that left her trembling, desire flaring like a raging inferno deep inside her. Gasping a helpless protest beneath his lips, she was left feeling strangely bereft as he slowly and reluctantly let her go.

They stared at each other in a long silence that appeared to last for ever. She could feel the heavy beat of his heart, his ragged breathing the only sound in the hushed atmosphere of the elegant room. With what seemed like the most enormous effort, she managed to twist away from his arms.

Giles rose to his feet and went over to gaze blindly down into the flames of the roaring log fire. 'I'm sorry. It seems that I've broken my promise to you.' He gave a long, weary sigh. 'You'd better go off to bed, Alicia, hmm? And don't worry,' he added bleakly, still with his back to her. 'You'll be quite safe from what you think of as my uncontrollable sexual appetite!'

His harsh, bitter laugh followed her down the long corridor, still seeming to echo in her ears as she climbed the wide flight of stairs to her bedroom.

She was still shivering, taut with nervous tension, as she sat down at the pretty dressing-table to brush her long hair, over half an hour later. Staring at her reflection in the mirror, she hardly recognised the pale wan face, nor the large, unhappy blue eyes full of unshed tears which shimmered with hard brilliance in the soft lamplight. Totally exhausted by the events of the day, she found that her tired brain couldn't seem to comprehend anything that Giles had said tonight. Her head, her body, her whole existence was aware of only one thing which dominated all thought and feeling. It was as if she had been struck by a thunderbolt as she finally realised the dreadful truth— that she still loved him. That, despite the intervening years, and her marriage to Walter, she could do nothing to retrieve her heart and her love, which she had once so unreservedly placed in Giles' hands.

CHAPTER EIGHT

ALICIA lay awake most of that night, tossing and turning as she tried to cope with the fact that, despite his betrayal in the past, and his present treacherous, underhand behaviour over the farm, she was still in love with Giles Ratcliffe.

Gripped by despair, she tried to think calmly about her feelings, but the words kept hammering in her brain: *Why him?* Why, of all the men in the world, should it be only Giles who set her pulses racing and her heart thudding in such a crazy rhythm? Every time she'd been in his presence since her return to Eastdale, she had felt an electric shock of overwhelming sensuality, and although she had tried to fool herself that it was merely sexual attraction, she now realised that it was far, far more than that.

The rest of the weekend passed in a blur, only briefly interspersed by the few occasions when she had to try and concentrate on the repairs to the damaged farmhouse.

Doing her very best to avoid all contact with Giles, she waited until he had left the Hall the next morning before asking Mr Renshaw to give her a lift back down to Winterfloods. There she found the plumber and his crew assessing the damage. Walking apathetically around the house, she was jerked from her self-absorption by the plumber informing her that he had instructions from Mr Ratcliffe.

'The squire says as how there ain't no hurry to put matters right,' he said. 'So I reckon me and the lads can see to the job the week after next, if that's all right with you, missis?'

'No, it certainly isn't all right with me!' she said grimly. 'I want a new boiler installed and those pipes mended as soon as possible.' If Giles thought he was going to keep her trapped up at the Hall, he was going to find out that he was sadly mistaken! 'I'm intending to move back into this house on Sunday night, and I want everything to be done by then. I know that you and your men don't usually work at the weekend, but . . .' she gave the man a wide, hopeful smile, 'I'm quite willing to pay time and a half, double time . . . or whatever it takes to get this job done. I'd also like you to draw up plans for a brand new system,' she added, sugaring the pill as the plumber hesitated, pushing back his cap and scratching his head as he looked around the filthy kitchen.

'And you'd be wanting me to do that work, as well?' he asked.

'Of course. Although I'm not in such a hurry to get that job done!' she grinned.

'Okay, missis, you've got yourself a deal,' he said, before turning to his men. 'Come on, boys. We's got a job to do—so look lively 'cos we ain't got much time.'

Alicia was still at the farmhouse when Edmund Truscott phoned. She had quite forgotten his invitation to dinner that night, but seized upon the welcome opportunity to avoid another evening meal at the Hall with Giles.

Poor Edmund, she hadn't been the best of companions. Unable to prevent herself from lapsing into long periods of silence, she knew she was being a boring companion, but there seemed very little she could do about it. She was sure that Edmund was as relieved as she was when the meal ended, and although he had surprisingly suggested that

he'd like to take her out again, she had been
deliberately vague about fixing a date.

There was nothing vague, however, about the
few words she had with Elsie when she visited her
cottage on Sunday morning. Stubborn as a mule,
the old housekeeper had announced her intention
of returning to the farm on Monday, only agreeing
to leave it to later in the week when Alicia pointed
out that she couldn't guarantee the plumbers would
be finished by then.

'For goodness' sake, stay at home in front of a
nice warm fire,' Alicia had urged. 'I'm not entirely
helpless in the kitchen, you know. In fact, I've
really enjoyed teaching myself to cook—even if I'm
not very good at it yet.'

'That's as maybe, but I don't feel right a-sitting
here doing of nothing. It ain't good for me—that I
do know.' Elsie's beady eyes had looked at Alicia
intently. 'I hear you was up at the Hall for tea.'

'Of course you did, Elsie! Quite honestly,' she
added as she got up to leave, 'I would be more than
grateful if you and your sister would give up this
stupid, nonsensical idea about Mr Ratcliffe and me
walking off into the sunset together. I know what
you've been plotting, so don't bother to deny it.
The telephone wires between this cottage and the
Hall must be red hot! As far as I can see, both you
and Mrs Renshaw are every bit as bad as Mrs
Jenkins.'

'That we're not!' Elsie had gasped with outrage
and injured innocence. 'All we's after is Mr
Ratcliffe's and your happiness. And it's 'bout time
you two stopped being right daft. You is both made
for each other, as us in the village do know, and
why you's both so blind . . . well, it fair beats me,
it does.'

There wasn't any answer to that, not unless she
was going to go into the long, involved history of
her relationship with Giles. So Alicia had merely

cautioned the older woman to keep warm, and hurriedly left her cottage.

Elsie was quite wrong about her and Giles being made for each other, Alicia thought later that night as she lay awake staring out of the window at the full moon. She'd had a long time, during all those years in London, to see that Giles had made the right decision as far as he was concerned. She hadn't liked Camilla, and for a long time after she had escaped to London, she had tortured herself with images of Giles making love to his fiancée. But as time had passed, Alicia had realised that at sixteen and a half she had been living in a fool's paradise. Camilla had been right for him. She had been to the right schools, knew the right people and had been used to acting as a hostess for her father. All of which admirably equipped her to be Giles' wife; in complete contrast to Alicia, who had been raised on a farm, knew hardly anyone other than the local farmers and the inhabitants of the neighbouring villages, and had never even attended a formal dinner party.

How foolish and so easily deceived she had been, all those years ago. How blindly she had believed Giles when he had talked of his wish to marry her. It only showed the depths of her childish naïveté, that she had seen nothing odd or peculiar in a man of twenty-six marrying a girl who wasn't yet seventeen. If Polly, when she had been the same age, had fallen for a man who was ten sophisticated years older than she was, Alicia knew she would have done her level best to prevent such a marriage taking place. Especially if, like Giles, the man in question had been busy making love to so many other girls at the same time!

Elsie had been half-way right, in one of the things she'd said. As a young girl, Alicia had clearly been as daft as a brush, but she was a lot older and wiser now. There was no way she was going to allow

herself, ever again, to be in a position where Giles
could hurt and wound her as he had done in the
past.

Moving carefully through the large rooms of the
Hall the next morning, she was relieved to find that
it seemed as if Giles was every bit as anxious to
avoid her company as she was to keep out of his
way. Dreading the thought of a formal Sunday
lunch, she persuaded Mrs Renshaw to make her up
a picnic lunch and a thermos of hot soup, under the
pretence of having to be at the farm to look after
the sheep, although she knew very well that there
was nothing she could do to make old Tom Bates
leave them in her care for the day. Realising that
Polly probably wouldn't return to the farm until
late afternoon, she spent the day boiling kettles of
hot water, so that she could scrub the floors and
wash the grimy soot from the walls of the farmhouse.
Unfortunately, the physical activity did little to
alleviate the tangled mass of confusion in her mind.

She realised that she'd burnt her bridges as far as
the farm was concerned. Committed to fighting
Giles for the tenancy was all very well, but that
decision had been taken before she had realised the
full truth of her emotional feelings for him. How on
earth was she going to cope, when she now knew
what torture lay in front of her?

The exuberant arrival back at the farm of Polly—
together with four geese and twelve chickens—put
paid to her dismal, introspective thoughts. The
plumbers had just finished their Herculean task as
Alicia showed her around the house, which was
more or less back to its original state. There was
still a lot of cleaning up to do, of course, and the
walls would need re-painting since, however hard
she scrubbed, she had failed to get rid of all the
greasy soot marks. It was only when they were
sitting in the kitchen having a cup of tea that Alicia
was able to broach the subject of Giles' eviction

notice, and the steps she was taking to gain the tenancy of the farm.

'What a double-dyed rat-fink that man's turned out to be!' Polly exclaimed. 'I don't really know him, of course, but I'd never have imagined that someone of his . . . well, of his standing in the community, would do something quite so underhand—not to say downright sneaky! And even if he was so desperate to get his hands on the farm, which doesn't seem very likely, I simply don't understand why he's never said a word about it to you.' She frowned in puzzlement. 'It all sounds most extraordinary and completely out of character, somehow. Especially since he's been so helpful over the sheep, and getting a plumber in here so quickly.'

'He probably sees that as protecting his property,' Alicia muttered grimly.

'But you told me he wasn't in a hurry to get the work done.' Polly gazed at her in bewilderment. 'Honestly, nothing seems to add up. Why don't you talk to him about it? I'm sure there must be a mistake somewhere.'

Alicia sighed and wearily shook her head. 'Both Mr Pemberton and Edmund Truscott said that was the very last thing I should do. Apparently I must leave Edmund to deal with Giles' agents, although I agree with you that it would be far better to be able to talk about it—calmly and quietly, if at all possible.'

'Anyway, I'm thrilled that we're going to be staying on here at the farm,' Polly said with a beaming smile, ignoring Alicia's warning that they weren't home and dry yet as she related, at great length, what a wonderful weekend she had spent with Bob's cousin.

'You seem to be seeing a lot of Bob Cooper. Are you—er—becoming quite keen on him?' Alicia asked carefully.

Polly grinned. 'Do I detect some stepmotherly concern?'

'No—of course not. I was only . . . well, taking an interest . . .' Alicia could feel her face flushing beneath Polly's amused gaze.

'Relax—I was only joking!' the younger girl laughed. 'Bob's just a nice guy, and I'm enjoying going out with him and learning more about farming. For instance, besides having a farm, his cousin also produces cheese from his herd of cows. It was tremendously interesting, and I'd love to have a go at doing the same thing,' she added wistfully.

'The geese and chickens are quite enough at the moment, thank you! If you want to make cheese, you'd better wait until you've done your agricultural training. One thing at a time, hmm?' Alicia gave her a wry smile as she slipped into a warm coat for the drive up to the Hall.

She didn't want to have to see Giles, but she couldn't just collect her case and slink off into the night without thanking him for his hospitality. When she found him in his sombre book-lined study, it proved to be a very fraught conversation, with both of them appearing to be tongue-tied and nervous. She was well aware of her own tenseness, but she was surprised to find the man she had always thought of as cool, smooth and sophisticated so oddly silent and abstracted. I might have been part of the wallpaper for all the notice he took of me! she thought angrily as she drove back to Winterfloods, and then realised just how ridiculous she was being. If, despite her own strong feelings for him, she had decided that any further contact would be a mistake, it was patently and stupidly illogical for her to moan about his sudden lack of interest.

Mentally and physically exhausted, she had fallen into bed that night, quite certain that she would never be able to close her eyes, only to wake the next morning from a deep, dreamless sleep.

'There isn't much post for you,' Polly said as she came downstairs. 'I wonder if Edmund Truscott has written to Giles yet? I'd love to be a fly on the wall when he gets *that* letter!'

But as they worked together, mucking out the animals and seeing to their hay and rations, the apprehension Alicia had felt at Polly's words gradually died away. It was bound to be days, maybe even weeks, before Giles heard about her claim from his land agents. Time enough to worry about it then.

An early lunch was followed by the arrival of Bob Cooper in his Volvo estate car, towing a horsebox.

'Are you going riding with Bob?' she looked at Polly in surprise.

'No. He's got to call on a nearby farmer,' Polly muttered quickly as she ran out to join the vet. 'Oh, by the way, I forgot to throw the hay down from the loft. I'll do it when I return, okay?'

'No, that's all right, I'll get on with it now,' said Alicia, waving them goodbye before climbing up the rickety old wooden ladder to the hay loft.

It was hard, physical labour, and Alicia welcomed it as an antidote to her bruised, emotional state. It was hot work, too. Not only the bodily exertion required to haul the bales over to the wide opening in the centre, far wall of the barn, which jutted out over the farmyard, and through which she threw the bales down into the yard; but considerable heat was generated by the calves and heifers in the barn below, rising through the wooden floor of the hay loft and contributing to the general warmth.

Her face glowing with exertion, Alicia discarded first her jacket and then the thick jumper she wore over a thin blue silk shirt. Her long, ash-blonde hair, tied by a loose bow at the back of her neck, soon came loose to fly about her head. She had just paused, removing some loose hay which had become caught in her long tresses, when she heard the roar of an engine, quickly followed by a screech of brakes and the loud bang of a car door. For a moment she stood startled, wondering who it could be, and then the blood turned to ice in her veins as she heard a violent shout down in the yard.

'Alicia . . .! Where in hell are you? *I'm going to murder you—you bloody girl!'*

Oh, dear lord! It was Giles, down there in the yard! There was only one thing which could be responsible for that shout of rage and fury, only one reason for the ferocious anger in his voice: he must have heard about her application for the tenancy of Winterfloods Farm!

Stiff with fright, Alicia held her breath, hoping against hope that when he received no reply to his hard, brutal knocking on the back door of the farmhouse, Giles would get into his car and go away. A few moments later, she realised that she was doomed to disappointment.

'It's no good trying to hide from me, Alicia,' he roared, the words echoing around the yard in the cold, still afternoon air. 'I know you're around here somewhere. And when I find you—by God, you're going to be sorry!'

Trembling, she looked about her with increasing fear and desperation. It wasn't just that she wanted to avoid discussing the tenancy business—she dared not! She'd always known that he would react violently when he learnt of her intentions, but she'd never imagined just how frightening the reality would be. No one in their right mind would want to face a man who sounded so set on murder and mayhem. But where could she hide? Other than trying to bury herself beneath the large stack of hay bales, the spacious loft offered no shelter at all.

Even the tall, upright wooden beams weren't thick enough to hide her slim figure. It was hopeless!

'Start saying your prayers—you're going to need them when I've finished with you!' Giles thundered. His voice, accompanied by the banging of barn and shed doors, was much louder now as he worked his way systematically—and inexorably—around the farmyard. As every minute passed, he was coming nearer and nearer to the cattle barn. She must escape! But how?

Almost paralysed by panic, Alicia spotted the trap door lying open on the far side of the loft floor. She couldn't do anything about the rickety wooden ladder; it was too long and too heavy for her to move. But maybe she could shut the trap door? Once she'd done that, Giles could batter away as much as he liked, but he wouldn't be able to break his way through, not if she managed to push home the ancient iron bolt. Even as she was formulating the plan, and long before she could put it into action, she realised from the harsh cry of triumphant laughter down below that she had left it far too late.

'*Gotcha!*' she heard Giles shout, and realised that he had only to look at the pile of hay bales lying down in the yard to work out exactly where she was hiding. A moment later her supposition was confirmed by the heavy thump of his feet on the rungs of the ladder, and a moment later his head and then his broad shoulders appeared through the opening in the floor.

'Aha! I thought I'd find you hiding up here!'

Too frightened to say anything for a moment, Alicia found her feet at last, backing nervously away as his powerful figure jumped up the last few rungs, and he stood regarding her in silence for a moment.

'Go away . . .!' she whispered, knowing even as

she did so, that he had no intention of listening to such a feebly voiced request. Nor did he.

'*Go away?*' he echoed, before giving a bitterly harsh, rasping laugh. 'You must be joking! You and I, my dear Alicia, have some talking to do, don't we . . .?' He advanced menancingly towards her trembling figure.

'No . . .!' she croaked, backing nervously towards the bales of hay.

'Why did you do it?' Giles demanded, his mouth in a hard tight line. '*Why didn't you tell me?* Why leave me to hear—in a phone call from my agents, for God's sake!—that you're claiming the tenancy of this farm?'

Alicia gasped, as much in reaction to the sheer audacity of his words as to his dark, menacing presence looming nearer every second.

'Cat got your tongue?' he taunted.

'Tell you? Why should I tell you anything?' she said with bitter scorn, finding her voice at long last.

He moved so fast and abruptly that she left it too late to get away from him, his hands grasping hold of her shoulders as he shook her violently. 'Don't you dare talk to me like that, you bitch! Yes, I said "bitch"—and I meant it!' he thundered as she flinched beneath his ever-tightening fingers. 'What else should I call you? Staying as a guest in my house, being so charming to the Renshaws, looking as if butter wouldn't melt in your mouth—while all the time you were planning to knife me in the back!' His voice rasped like rough sandpaper on stone. 'My God, I don't think I've ever been so angry, not in all my born days!'

'Angry!' She gave a shrill, hysterical laugh, glaring up at him with defiance flashing from her brilliant blue eyes. 'You're not the only one who's angry. I've been furious with your bloody-minded behaviour towards me for most of the past week. So why shouldn't you have a dose of your own medicine?'

His eyes narrowed to dark grey points of hard steel, piercing her as she stood shivering before him. 'What the hell are you talking about?' he demanded harshly. 'What bloody-minded behaviour . . .? Giving you the use of my shepherd? Rescuing you from a broken-down car and getting it mended? Trying to help you all I could? Is that what you call "bloody-minded"?' he snarled at her. 'If so, then let me tell you, you have no idea of *just* how bloody-minded I can be!'

'I don't need you to tell me!' she lashed back angrily. 'When your damned land agents served me with a "notice to quit" this farm by Lady Day, I knew *just* what sort of man you are. You couldn't even tell me to my face, could you? Three short weeks—that's all you gave me. Three weeks to leave a house my family have lived in for generations!' she shouted, finally and completely losing her temper.

Giving him a mighty kick on the shins, she wrenched her body away from beneath his hands, hitting him across the face so hard that it sounded like a gun shot. Giles froze, his heavy breathing the only sound in the large hay loft as Alicia stared in horror at the livid red marks of her fingers on his pale cheek. She'd never hit anyone before, and she was completely shattered at her action. How could she? What on earth had possessed her to do such a thing?

'I—I'm desperately sorry . . .' she whispered, quickly backing away from his threatening figure. 'I really didn't mean—*Ow . . .!*' she gave a sharp cry as she stumbled backwards over a loose bale of hay, losing her balance and falling breathless on to the wooden floor. As she lay winded for a moment, Alicia's face burned with humiliation beneath Giles' cold, contemptuous smile which rubbed salt into the wounds of her bitter hurt and anger.

'What's all this nonsense about a "notice to quit"?' he demanded curtly.

Struggling to raise herself from the hay, Alicia quickly subsided when he took a threatening step towards her. 'What a bastard you are!' she grated huskily. 'It's just like you to pretend to know nothing about it. I'd hardly returned to this village when your damned land agents served my solicitor with that eviction notice. I—I couldn't believe it! I couldn't believe you'd do that to me . . . and never say a word. God! what a fool I was!' she panted angrily.

'I had absolutely nothing to do with any eviction notice,' he retorted. 'I give you my word of honour, Alicia, that this is the first I've heard of it.'

'Your word of honour? *Don't make me laugh!*' she jeered. 'You always were such a liar, Giles Ratcliffe. You've lied to me as long as I've known you, so I'm sure as hell not going to believe you now!'

He swore violently, his eyes flashing with anger. 'For God's sake, you stupid woman, I'm telling you the truth!'

'You can shout at me as much as you like. It won't make a scrap of difference to me. You just wait! I'm going to win the tenancy of Winterfloods, if it's the last thing I do!' she taunted as he stared down at her in silence.

She glared back at him as his gaze moved slowly over her body, almost able to feel the scorching heat from his grey eyes, now gleaming as they surveyed her breasts, thrown into thrusting prominence as she leaned back on her elbows. Even as she tried to comprehend the whirling messages of alarm in her brain, his features seemed to alter, the harsh planes and angles of his face softening in an indefinable manner, but one to which her body instantly responded. She could feel an ache deep in the pit of her stomach, her pulses hammering with an insistent, fast rhythm that echoed the pounding of her heart.

'No . . .!' she whispered huskily, scrambling awkwardly to her feet and making an instinctive dash for the trap door. She only managed to take three strides before his arm flashed out to catch and hold her arm, swiftly jerking her towards him. The arrested momentum of her body gave it an extra weight as she cannoned back into his tall frame, the impact sending them both flying to the ground. Giles was the first to recover, rolling over to grab her wrists and forcing them back over her head as he pinned her to the mound of soft hay.

Alicia's heart sank as she realised she was trapped. Not only had she lost control of her hands, but Giles was lying half across her body, and although she desperately tried to wriggle out from beneath his heavy weight, her exertions were in vain, merely leaving her exhausted and almost crying with frustration. 'Let . . . me . . . go . . .!' she panted, the breath rasping in her lungs as she fought for breath, trembling violently as his dark head came down towards her.

The bruising force of his mouth crushed hers in a long, scorching kiss of rampant possession, the relentless pressure forcing her lips apart, his tongue plundering the inner softness of her mouth in a devastating invasion of her shattered senses. When at last he released her numb, swollen mouth she gasped for air, whispering bitterly, 'You—you've hurt me!'

'I meant to,' he ground out through clenched teeth as he stared down at her pale cheeks. Time seemed suspended as she saw the dark pupils of his eyes slowly enlarge, glowing feverishly as they moved over her trembling lips and the cloud of ash-blonde hair flowing over the soft, meadow-sweet hay.

'Oh, Alicia . . .! I wish to God I knew what we're

supposed to be fighting about,' he murmured huskily as she stared helplessly back at him, dazed and hypnotised by the intensity of his glinting grey eyes. 'But just at the moment . . .' a sound broke from his throat, half-way between a laugh and a groan, as he lowered his mouth to hers, effectively smothering her wild cry of protest.

There was no denying that it was what she had been hungering for, and yet dreading, for so long. As Giles' lips took possession of hers, her mind was still continuing the fight, although her weak body responded eagerly to the mouth moving over her bruised lips with insidious persuasion, gently forcing and probing them apart with a sensual warmth that inflamed her senses. Desperately trying to cling on to her sanity, Alicia could feel a forceful tide of desire sweeping through her body, and knew she was betrayed by the deep compulsion to respond to her overwhelming need of him.

A soft moan broke from her throat as she yielded to the possession of his mouth, the sound provoking a shuddering convulsion in the body lying over hers. Letting go of her wrists, Giles ran his hand over the curve of her breast and on down to the swell of her hips, the scorching path of his fingers seeming to burn through her clothes.

Raising his head, he stared searchingly down at her with eyes that blazed fiercely in the dim light of the hay loft, cupping her face with hands that shook and trembled with barely controlled tension. 'I've got to have you, Alicia,' he rasped hoarsely. 'Eight long years I've hungered for you . . . it's more than flesh and blood can stand!' he groaned, burying his face in the deep valley of her breasts.

A deep, responsive shudder tore through her body, her arms closing about him, her fingers curling into his thick dark hair as he pressed feverish kisses over her soft skin. She wanted him. There was nothing in the world she wanted more than the possession of this man, to have his hands and lips caressing her . . . Racked by desire, she felt the thought of his lovemaking cause her body to burn and shake, her need of him so intense that it was like a deep physical pain.

Firmly in the grip of an elemental, primitive force that was quite beyond either of them to control, he tore the clothes first from her body and then his. She felt no shame or regret as her hands moved over the strong contours of his body, the flesh beneath her fingers so achingly, poignantly familiar. And then there was no more time to think, to consider or to draw back as the raw, savage emotion which had been repressed for so long exploded passionately between them, their bodies merging in the wild, untamed hunger of their overpowering need for each other.

Later, as they lay warmly and drowsily entwined together, almost buried in the sweet-scented hay, she felt Giles' fingers moving softly over her cheek to gently turn her face towards him. 'We must talk, darling,' he murmured.

'Mmm . . .?' Alicia blinked sleepily. She was still dazed by the passion which had leapt between them, incredulous at the force of her own reaction to his frenzied lovemaking. It was as if some wild spirit had taken possession of her mind and body, releasing a fire in her blood which had raged totally out of control. Soaring upward to the heavens like a shooting star, it had seemed incredible that she could know such consummate joy as she gloried in his passionate lovemaking. But just as with all fiercely burning meteors, she was now swiftly falling back down to earth, and having to face harsh reality was almost more than she could bear.

'I'm not going to apologise for what's just happened,' he said quietly. 'It was inevitable, wasn't it? I want you—and this time I'm not going to let you go!'

She shivered at the flat, hard determination in his voice, and the dominant touch of his hand as he caressed the soft curves of her naked body. The barriers she had erected over the years had fallen too fast, too violently, and it terrified her to know how completely she had given herself away, betraying her love for the man lying beside her. The sexual magnetism between them was as explosive and unstable as dynamite, only requiring the lightest touch of the fuse to once more destructively blow her life apart.

She turned her head away, clamping her eyelids shut to prevent him from seeing the weak, hopeless tears that threatened to fall any minute. She had to be strong. She must shut him out of her life, and yet she could already feel desire flicking into life again as his fingers moved erotically over her breasts. 'No . . . we can't . . .' she muttered helplessly. 'We mustn't . . . ever again . . .'

'Are you crazy?' he demanded, gathering her roughly into his embrace and fiercely pressing his lips to the base of her throat as she struggled in his arms. 'Don't fight me any more, Alicia,' he groaned thickly. 'I need you! There's never been anyone else for me. I want to marry you and . . .' the rest of his words were lost as he jerked his head upwards, swearing under his breath as they both heard a vehicle draw into the farmyard.

There was the noise of a car door banging, and then Polly's indignant voice, 'That looks like Giles Ratcliffe's Range Rover. Honestly! Fancy leaving it parked bang in the middle of the yard, so that no one can get past it!' Her harsh, caustic tones were followed by Bob's quiet murmur, and a rattling sound as he lowered the back of the horse box on to the ground.

'That damned girl should have been strangled at birth!' Giles swore hoarsely, before leaping to his feet, sweeping up his clothes which were lying in disarray on the bales of hay, and putting them on with quick, efficient movements of his tense body.

Alicia stared at him in a horrified daze, so shocked by Polly's unexpected return that for a moment she forgot her own nakedness, her mind and body paralysed by cold fear and apprehension. And then she, too, was scrambling for her clothes, impeded by the trembling of her hands as she struggled to do up the buttons of her shirt.

'For God's sake, hurry!' he whispered over his shoulder as he went across the floor to peer down into the yard below, before coming back, his shoulders heaving with silent laughter. 'You're going to love this,' he said softly, grinning as he picked strands of hay from the wild confusion of her hair. 'Your dear stepdaughter has arrived back with, if I'm not mistaken, what looks remarkably like two Jersey cows!'

'What . . .?' she stared at him in amazement, before she realised that Polly's latest acquisitions were the very least of her problems. 'What are we going to do?' she moaned helplessly, leaning against his hard, firm body for a moment as she tried to bring some sort of cohesive order to her dazed mind.

'Frankly, darling, I don't think that there is much we can do.' His mouth curved with amusement as he gazed down at her dishevelled appearance. 'We both look such a mess that all we can hope to achieve is to try and carry the whole thing off with as much panache as possible,' he added softly, brushing some of the hay from her thick sweater. 'I suggest our best course of action is for me to shin down the ladder and engage the young couple in conversation, while you slip into the house.'

'I can't! It won't work—they're bound to see me . . .!' moaned Alicia, dreading the thought of having to face Polly's incredulous eyes and searching questions. How could she possibly even begin to explain what had happened? 'And . . . and we haven't talked about the tenancy business,' she added helplessly.

'That can wait,' he said firmly. 'I can only think my land agents must have jumped the gun. I certainly never gave them any instructions to evict you—and it completely beats me why you ever imagined that I'd do such a thing.'

'Well . . . I—I could hardly believe it at first, but . . .'

Giles gave her a quick hug. 'Of course I don't want you living at Winterfloods. It was only because I thought you were seriously intending to do so—and you hadn't told me—that I went berserk. Besides, the whole matter is totally unimportant now. When we get married, you'll be living up at the Hall with me,' he murmured, giving her a swift kiss before striding over to the trap door. 'Wish me luck!' He gave a low laugh as he disappeared down the ladder into the cattle barn below.

Alicia stared after him with blank, dazed eyes, only recalled from her trance-like state by the sound of laughter below in the yard, and the roar of an engine as Giles obviously made good his escape. Which was more than she was going to be able to do, she realised as she climbed back down the ladder, and met Polly leading one of her new Jersey cows into the barn.

There was a long silence as Polly looked at her, and then turned her head to glance back over her shoulder as if searching for Giles' tall figure, before looking at Alicia again. Her green eyes widened as she viewed the dishevelled state of her stepmother's clothes, which were completey covered in strands of hay, as was the disorderly length of her tangled, ash-blonde hair.

A deep tide of crimson swept over Alicia's face as she saw Polly's mouth twitch with amusement. 'Well, well, what have you been up to? I know it's the wrong time of year, but it definitely looks as if you've got hay fever!'

Alicia felt almost faint with embarrassment. Taking a deep breath, she looked the girl straight in the eye. 'I—I'm not prepared to discuss the matter,' she said, but the words which should have sounded firm and impressive issued from her mouth in a faint, croaking whisper.

'Okay, okay—my lips are sealed.' Polly's shoulders shook with suppressed laughter. 'After all, I suppose it's certainly *one* way for you and Giles to settle that tenancy business!'

CHAPTER NINE

ALICIA'S tall, slender figure walked slowly down the steps of the London hospital, across the forecourt busy with the arrival and departure of ambulances, and over to where Simpson was waiting beside the Rolls.

'Mrs Simpson seemed very much better today,' she said as the chauffeur opened the rear door of the vehicle. 'Are you sure I can't persuade you to change your mind? I'll be quite happy to wait here while you pop up and see her.'

'Thank you, madam, but I'll be seeing my wife tonight, and I know she finds having more than one visitor at a time rather exhausting.' He gave a wry smile. 'Both our daughters and their husbands turned up last night, and she was looking very tired by the time they left.'

Poor Mrs Simpson, Alicia thought, settling back on the leather seat as the Rolls moved smoothly out of the car park and into the busy London traffic. The operation itself had gone perfectly smoothly, but she was still feeling very weak. In fact, she had been somewhat tearful when Alicia had visited her yesterday, worrying about the long convalescence necessary after such a major operation. However, Alicia's assurance that there was no problem, since she and Polly were likely to be staying on at the farm for the foreseeable future, had done much to reassure the housekeeper.

'I want you to have a good long holiday,' Alicia had said when visiting her just now. 'And stop worrying about how I'm managing on my own, down here in London, because while I've been up in Shropshire, I've been teaching myself how to cook.' A statement that produced a broad smile from Mrs Simpson.

'For goodness' sake, don't make me laugh, madam— it's these stitches, I only have to cough for them to act up something chronic!'

Why on earth did everyone seem to laugh whenever she mentioned teaching herself to cook? Alicia wondered. Even Mrs Renshaw and Elsie had both appeared to find the fact highly amusing, although Polly had been very complimentary over her efforts. Polly! The girl never ceased to surprise her . . . Alicia sighed, leaning back and turning her head to stare blindly out at the passing traffic.

Almost two weeks ago, after she and Giles had been more or less caught *in flagrante delicto* in the hay loft, she had stumbled across the farmyard and into the house feeling absolutely shattered. Quite apart from all other considerations, she had been worried sick about what on earth she could say to Polly. How could she possibly explain what had happened? Of course, Polly was almost twenty-one years of age but, even so, there were few girls who could be expected to view their stepmother's clear lack of moral fibre with anything other than a very jaundiced eye. She had obviously forfeited any respect Polly might have had for her, and she very much feared that their easy, fond relationship would now be a thing of the past. She was sitting in her bedroom feeling as miserable as sin, with phrases like 'disgraceful behaviour' and 'disgusting conduct' running through her tired brain, when there had been a knock on the door and Polly had come into the room.

'What are you doing, sitting up here in the dark?' she had demanded, switching on the bedside lights.

'God, you look awful! You haven't been crying, have you?'

'No—of course not . . .' Alicia muttered, fiercely blowing her nose and surreptitiously trying to wipe the tears from her eyes.

'Hmm . . . It certainly looks as if you've been have a good howl. I thought that now . . . well, you and Giles . . .'

'It—it's nothing to do with him—not really,' Alica sighed. 'It's all my fault. I'm sorry, Polly, I—I can't defend myself, and I know what you must think.'

Polly smiled. 'What I *think* is that I'm surprised it hasn't happened before now. Honestly, Ally,' she went on as her stepmother looked up at her in astonishment, 'I'm not entirely blind, you know! It's been glaringly obvious to me—and I imagine to everyone else as well—that Giles fancies you rotten. And from the way you sort of "hum" whenever he's around, I guess the feeling is entirely mutual!'

'But . . . but don't you mind? I mean . . .'

'Why on earth should I mind?'

'Well—er—it's not exactly—um—that is, I'm supposed to be . . .'

'My whiter-than-white stepmother?' Polly grinned. 'Come off it, Ally! You're only four years older than I am, and hardly ready for a lace cap and a rocking chair just yet. Okay, I'll admit that if I didn't like the guy, I might well feel differently,' she added seriously. 'But Elsie has always said that you two have been in love with each other since the year dot—she's been quite lyrical on the subject, in fact.' She paused. 'You *do* love him, I take it?'

The long curtain of her ash-blonde hair hid Alicia's burning face as she nodded, grabbing her handkerchief to blow her nose again.

'So where's the problem—and why the tears? You'll get married and live happily ever after—end of story!'

Alicia continued to stare down at the floor. 'It's nothing like as simple as that,' she muttered.

'Why not? Doesn't he want to marry you?'

'Yes . . . no . . . oh, it's far too complicated for me to explain everything,' Alicia sighed heavily, getting up and going over to sit down at her dressing-table, and grimacing at her pale, tear-stained face in the mirror. 'The fact is, Polly, that there's a whole chunk of the past that Giles and I haven't talked about, and . . . and we didn't even get the tenancy business sorted out. All he said was that his agents had "jumped the gun", and he knew nothing about the eviction notice.'

'I knew it! I never thought he'd do something so awful. Surely you must have known that it was entirely out of character? I mean, he's the sort of guy who prides himself on "doing the right thing", isn't he?'

Alicia picked up a brush, dragging it roughly through her hair. 'Irrespective of how I feel about the man, there are a lot of other factors involved. It isn't just what happened between us in the past—and I don't think I'd ever trust him again after that—or the question over the future of this farm. Giles has also got a mistress hanging around. He more or less said that he was only using her to make me jealous, but . . .'

'What's she like?'

Alicia's lips tightened. 'I suspect her of having all the morals of an alley cat, and the appetite of a man-eating shark. However, honesty compels me to state that she is also stunningly beautiful. Not to mention her voluptuous figure, which would make page three of the *Sun* newspaper without any trouble,' she added gloomily.

'Well, you're beautiful, and I bet she isn't nearly as nice as you are, Ally.'

Alicia managed a shaky grin. 'I appreciate your loyalty, kid. However, this whole business between Giles and myself is far too complicated to be sorted out as easily as you seem to think. The fact is, Polly,

I don't trust him, and that's a basic requirement for any relationship. So, please let's just drop the subject, shall we?'

As she lay in bed later that night, Alicia's mind see-sawed back and forth. She wasn't sixteen and innocent as a young puppy, as she'd been all those years ago. She was now twenty-four, a grown woman, and she knew what had happened to her. For the moment she'd been forced to stay on at the farm, she'd known that Giles possessed a black magic as far as she was concerned. She had been right to be wary and afraid of him, because she'd instinctively known that if she was ever to experience his lovemaking again, she was never going to be satisfied with just that one occasion. And she had been quite right. Even now, her body was burning for his touch, her crying need for him so intense that it amounted almost to a physical pain.

It was a pain that didn't diminish during the days that followed, the agony intensified by the humiliating fact that Giles hadn't, as he had promised, got in touch with her after the episode in the hay loft. It was two days before she received a phone call from Renshaw, to say that Mr Ratcliffe had been suddenly called away abroad to Australia, and Renshaw didn't know when he would return.

A long, unhappy week had gone by when Alicia decided to go down to the lower meadows to inspect the old stone outbarn. It would soon be time to put the heifers out to grass, but they would need supplementary feeding and she had to make sure that the barn contained enough hay. Sitting on some bales, with only the occasional cooing of a pigeon up in the rafters to break the silence, she forced herself to recognise the truth behind that passionate encounter between Giles and herself. She had demonstrated— once again—that she was every bit the willing victim that she had been eight years ago. While as for Giles . . .? He hadn't changed one iota. There might well be an extraordinarily strong sexual bond between them, but it would be totally naïve of her to assume that he wasn't able to have the same successful relationship with other woman. For 'Alicia today,' read 'Melanie tomorrow' . . . she thought bitterly. If she'd had any lingering doubt of his complete insincerity and self-satisfaction, it had been firmly banished by his conspicuous flight abroad. And yet . . . She buried her face in the soft, sweet-smelling hay, trying to control the sobs which shook her slender body. Despite everything, she was still in love with Giles, her body on fire for his touch with a desperate longing that filled every fibre of her being.

Eventually managing to pull herself together, she slowly made her way back to the farm to be met by Polly with the news that Giles had just phoned from Australia.

'It was a terribly bad line, and I only caught just a few words of what he was saying. From what I could gather, there've been floods in something called the Murray River area . . .? Anyway, he's going to telephone tomorrow.'

'Really?' Alicia shrugged. 'I don't think I'm particularly interested one way or another.'

'Really . . .?' Polly echoed, her voice heavy with disbelief. 'Well, in that case, I don't suppose that you'll be interested to hear that we have a Mrs Melanie Todd sitting in the kitchen?'

'What . . .? What on earth is she doing here?'

Polly shook her head. 'I haven't a clue. But from your description—which was spot on, by the way—I take it that she's Giles' little hot water bottle . . .?'

'For God's sake, Polly, don't be so crude!' Alicia snapped, before she gave a heavy sigh. 'Sorry—yes, you're quite right. She is—er—Giles' girl-friend. And she would turn up when I'm looking such a mess, wouldn't she?' she sighed again. 'I suppose I'd better go and see what she wants.'

Melanie, it transpired, didn't want anything. In

fact, it wasn't till later that Alicia came to the conclusion that the woman had been bored, and felt like sharpening her nails on someone. Rather like a child who quite intentionally unravels her mother's knitting, Melanie clearly took pleasure in being deliberately destructive.

The next half-hour was, as Alicia had feared it would be, fairly horrific. Melanie's first remark set the tone. 'Oh, dear, silly little me—I'm far too overdressed for a visit to a farm!' Her words were accompanied by a tinkling laugh and a raised eyebrow at Alicia's muddy jeans and ancient, straw-covered sweater as she slipped off her red fox fur coat to reveal an expensive cream silk dress. After which, the visit proceeded to go rapidly downhill.

The dark girl continued with her brilliant smile and artless chatter, planting stinging barbs in Alicia's hide with all the technical skill of a professional knife thrower. And when Polly loyally tried to intervene on her behalf, she only made matters worse, forcing Alicia to give her a swift, warning kick beneath the kitchen table. Polly took the hint, but as she lapsed into a sullen silence, glaring at Melanie with stormy green eyes, Alicia's nerves were at screaming pitch when the sudden ring of the telephone came to her rescue. Jumping thankfully to her feet, she mumbled an excuse and hurried from the room. When she came back into the kitchen some minutes later, she saw that Melanie had left.

'I see she's gone, thank God,' she smiled wanly at Polly.

'I simply don't understand why you didn't make more of a fight of it! That woman has all the charm of deadly nightshade and poison ivy—I mean, she's absolutely horrendous!'

Alicia gave an unhappy shrug. 'There really wasn't any point, you know. Once you start trading insults with someone like that, you only drag yourself down to their level.' She began to collect up the tea cups. 'I must say I thought she was here to stay—what made her take herself off so sharply?'

Polly laughed. 'Well, I'm afraid it was your phone call that did it. I told her it was bound to be Giles, and how much I was looking forward to him coming back, because he was soon going to be my new stepfather . . .!'

'Oh, God!'

'Do you know, that's *exactly* what Melanie said, before she tore out of the house!'

'Well, for your information, that wasn't Giles on the phone—it was Simpson,' Alicia said grimly, failing for once to appreciate Polly's sense of humour. 'Apparently Mrs Simpson has been taken into hospital for an urgent operation.

'Oh, I'm so sorry. I do hope she's going to be all right.'

'I'm sure she will. From what her husband said, I rather gathered that she's undergoing a hysterectomy. But I think I'll drive down to London tonight, just to make sure she's being properly looked after.'

Alicia had been glad to leave the farm, and Mrs Simpson's operation proved to be the perfect excuse. At least it didn't look as if she was deliberately running away from her problem, and it would give her some time to look at the events of the past weeks, and get them into some sort of perspective . . .

'Will you be needing the car tonight, madam?' Simpson's voice broke into her thoughts, and she looked up to see that they had arrived back at the large house in Belgravia.

'No, I won't need it. And since I'm not planning to do anything tomorrow, why don't you take a few days off? I can manage perfectly well on my own, and I think you ought to spend a lot more time with your wife.'

It took her some time to persuade the chauffeur that she could actually exist without any servants in the house, and she suddenly realised just how much she had enjoyed living at the farm. Despite the ever-present problem of Giles, her life had been far more free and purposeful. Whatever happened in the future, she knew that she never wanted to live permanently in London again.

She was down in the large kitchen, making herself an omelette, when Polly rang as she'd done every night since Alicia had been away. 'How are things at the farm?' she asked, perching herself on a stool by the phone extension which hung on the wall of the kitchen.

'Everything's fine. Mr Bates says all the lambs are okay, and if the weather holds the sheep can all go back out into the paddock next week. By the way, Giles rang again, after I'd spoken to you yesterday. Apparently he's on his way back from Australia.'

'You didn't tell him where I was, did you?' Alicia asked anxiously.

'Honestly, Ally! Would I do that, when you'd already told me not to mention the fact?'

'No, I'm sorry. It's just . . . well, I need a lot more time to think, that's all.'

Alicia thought that Polly had muttered something along the lines of too much thinking being a bad idea, but as she'd had to hang up quickly when she smelt her omelette burning on the stove, she wasn't entirely sure.

It must have been Polly's reminder of Giles that was the reason for it taking her so long to fall asleep, she told herself as she tossed restlessly in her bed that night. If only she could have fallen in love with someone like Scott Harper, or any of the other attractive men she had met after Walter's death, many of whom had clearly demonstrated their interest in being more than friends. Someone with whom she could have lived a quiet life, well away from the turbulent memories of the past. It was completely beyond her comprehension to understand how it was possible to be so helplessly in love with a man, and at the same time violently disapprove of his lifestyle. Leopards couldn't change their spots, she thought sadly, and it was highly unlikely that Giles would prove to be the exception to the rule.

She had only just dropped off to sleep when it seemed she was awakened by a violent banging on the front door, which echoed loudly through the house. Turning over to gaze sleepily at her bedside clock, Alicia saw that it was two o'clock in the morning. She was just about to turn over, burying her head beneath the pillows and trying to get back to sleep, when she suddenly thought that it might be Simpson. Maybe his wife had taken a sudden turn for the worse?

Quickly jumping out of bed, she threw on a thin wrap and hurried down the stairs, and through the large hall towards the door. Pulling back the bolts, she opened it—only to try and slam it quickly shut again as her dazed, sleepy eyes saw who was standing on the step.

'Oh, no, you don't!' Giles said, giving the door a hard push, and forcing his way past her to dump a large suitcase on the black and white marble floor.

'What on earth do you think you're doing?' she demanded, shivering in the draught of cold night air. 'Get out of my house, immediately!'

'Like hell I will!' he retorted, closing and bolting the front door behind him. 'I've just flown in from Melbourne—and that means almost twenty-four hours in a damned aeroplane. I slept most of the way, so I haven't got jet-lag, but I do have an almighty thirst. So I'm sorry to say that I'm not after your body . . . well, not just at the moment. What I really *need*, my darling, is a very, very strong drink. You're not going to refuse me that, surely?'

Alicia glared up at him and then gave a heavy sigh. He did look unusually tired and exhausted, in fact there was an almost haggard look in his face. 'All right,' she said at last. 'Just one drink, and that's it.'

'If you say so,' he murmured, following her through the hall and into a room lined with books, where a fire was still burning in the grate. 'This is nice,' he said, sinking thankfully into a large leather chair and looking around as Alicia went over to a table. 'Whisky, please—neat,' he added, leaning back and putting his feet up on the fender.

'Anything else you require?' she asked acidly as she came over to place the glass in his hands.

'Not just at the moment,' he drawled, his eyes sweeping over her thin dressing-gown, which did little to hide the transparent silk nightdress nor the warm curves of her body.

'Hurry up with that drink,' she snapped, her cheeks reddening as she clutched the gown closely about her. 'I'm tired, and want to go to bed.'

'That's the best suggestion I've heard all week.' He drained his glass and eased himself out of the chair. 'Well, what are we waiting for?' he asked, as she looked at him in confusion.

'I don't . . .'

Giles sighed. 'Come on, Alicia. You want your bed—and believe me, so do I!' He walked over to open the door.

'Just a minute,' she said quickly as he disappeared into the hall. 'Come back here at once! Where do you think you're going?' she shouted as she saw him taking the stairs two at a time. 'If you think that I'm putting up with this sort of nonsense . . .!' She ran swiftly up the stairs after him, realising with a sinking heart that he would have no difficulty in knowing which room was hers, since it was the only one with its door open and she had left her bedside lamp on.

Sure enough, there he was—stretched out on his back on her big double bed! He must have moved like greased lightning to get there so swiftly, but that wasn't important, she told herself as she stood in the doorway fuming with rage. Far more to the point was the question: how was she to get rid of him?

'Okay, Giles. It's been a great joke, but now it's over. I want you up and out of here—*immediately!*' she commanded angrily, almost stamping her bare feet with frustration when he didn't move a muscle. He might have been tired, but he couldn't possibly have gone off to sleep that quickly . . . or could he? Striding over towards the bed, she stared down at his recumbent form. 'I know you're not asleep, you foul man!' she stormed. 'Wake up, or I—*ah . . .!*'

One minute she had been giving him a rough shake, and the next she felt her arms grasped as she was quickly pulled down on top of him. 'I knew you couldn't keep your hands off my body,' he mocked softly, rolling over to pin her slender form beneath him. 'Umm . . . you smell delicious,' he added, pressing his warm lips to the soft hollow at the base of her throat.

'You deliberately tricked me,' she protested. 'And God knows how you got around Polly, because she's the only one who knows I'm here. You've no right to behave like this,' she breathed huskily, trying to hang on to her concentration as his lips moved on down over her skin towards the firm swell of her breasts.

'I had every right. You're as slippery as an eel, and if I gave you half a chance, you'd slip off the hook and wriggle away for ever. I wasn't going to let that happen again,' Giles retorted, lifting his head to gaze down into her blue eyes. 'It's been a hell of a week. I arrived home after making love to you in the hay loft to find that the manager of a farm I own out in Australia had died of a sudden heart attack, leaving a wife and four children under ten years of age. He and his wife were personal friends of mine, and I had no choice but to fly out there as quickly as I could, and to try and sort out any problems.' He gave a heavy sigh. 'What with trying to comfort the family, find a temporary manager, *and* trying to phone you when most of the lines in North Victoria appeared to

be out of action, I've been nearly out of my mind,'
he growled.

Alicia closed her eyes as she tried to absorb what
he'd been saying. He hadn't deliberately walked out
on her, after all. But that fact didn't really alter the
basic problems between them . . .

He lay staring down at her in silence for a moment,
his eyes narrowing to glittering grey points of steel.
'Look at me!' he commanded, her eyes flying open
with apprehension at the harsh note in his voice. 'As
far as I'm concerned, the last weeks since you
returned to Eastdale have been sheer, unadulterated
hell. And I won't pretend that the last eight years
have been much better.' He paused, the harsh lines
of his face emphasised by a faint flush spreading over
his cheekbones as he took a deep breath. 'I love you,
Alicia, and I want you to be my wife.'

'No!' She trembled beneath his hard body, shaking
her head. 'No, I can't . . . you can't . . . it's no good.
It would never work. It's—well, you must see that it's
quite impossible!'

'What's impossible? The fact that I love you? My
dearest one, I can't remember a time when I didn't
love you,' he said in a voice of such deep intensity
that she almost choked on a hard lump in her throat.
'I want you to marry me. I want to spend the rest of
my days with you—and loving you.' He put a hand
beneath her chin, gently forcing her to look at him,
and brushing the hair from her face. 'Just for the
moment, I want you to forget the past. I want you to
forget your late husband and my ex-wife, and all the
lies and deceits which have been practised upon us
both. We can—and will—talk about it all later,' he
said firmly. 'However, there is only one thing that
really matters, only one simple fact that has any
relevance at all. Alicia, I must know the truth! I love
you, and I think—I'm almost sure—that you love me.
Am I right?' he asked, the hand holding her chin
shaking with tension as his eyes devoured her face.

'I . . . it's not that simple . . . you can't expect . . .'
Her blue eyes slid away from his intense gaze.

'Yes or no?' he demanded hoarsely.

Her lips trembled, and her mouth was suddenly
dry. 'All right! Yes—damn it! Yes, I love you . . .'
she wailed. 'And . . . and I wish to hell I didn't!'

'Oh, my darling . . .!' he breathed, his hands
framing her face as he lowered his head to hungrily
possess her lips. It was always the same, she thought
helplessly as desire ran like swift mercury through her
veins. Whatever they said or did to each other, and
despite all the unhappiness in the past, Giles had
only to touch her to ignite a raging fire that burned
with a white-hot heat.

'It's no good . . . it's all quite impossible,' she
breathed as his lips left hers to trail a scorching path
down her neck, pressing soft kisses in the warm, deep
cleft of her breasts.

'Nothing is impossible,' he whispered thickly against
her skin, his fingers gently brushing aside both her
wrap and the thin lace straps of her nightgown, to
expose the rounded curves of her breasts to his view.

'No, Giles . . . This doesn't solve anything . . .' she
gasped, although she made no move to stop him from
removing her garments, the soft touch of his mouth
and hands moving over her flesh becoming more
insistent, more possessively arousing.

'You're quite wrong—it's the answer to everything!'
he muttered, peeling off his clothes and clasping her
naked form to his hard masculine body. His hoarse
voice was almost the last thing she heard, as she sank
down beneath the tidal waves of feverish, passionate
desire. Fierce tremors of pleasure zig-zagged like
lightning through her body, each lingering caress,
each erotic and intimate touch, leaving her aching
with the intensity of her need for his possession.
Quivering with ecstasy, she was lost to all sense of
reality, only aware of a wild exultation in his
passionate, thrusting possession and her own frenzied

response, before the world seemed to disintegrate around them in fragments of light and power.

She must have been dreaming, Alicia thought, opening her sleepy eyes to see the pale morning sun shining in through her windows. A moment later harsh, glaring reality dispelled the languorous mists in her brain, and she struggled to sit up, staring with horror at the clothes strewn around the room.

'Relax, Alicia!' She turned to see Giles standing in the doorway which led to her bathroom. He had shaved, his hair still damp from the shower as, with only a short towel tied casually around his hips, he regarded her with a warm smile. 'I love you. You love me—and we're going to be married. Remember?' he murmured, walking over to the bed and sitting down to put his warm arms about her.

'No, please . . .!' she gasped as he trailed his lips over her breasts. 'You can't . . .'

'Oh, yes I can . . .!' he murmured huskily, his mouth closing over first one swollen nipple and then the other, causing her to moan helplessly beneath the torment of his lips and tongue.

'Please . . . Giles . . .' she gasped. 'We must be—be sensible,' she added huskily, forcing herself to push him away as she struggled to sit up in the bed. 'I may have said that I love you . . .' her cheeks flushed, and she tried to wriggle away from his fingers which were drawing patterns on the inside of her thigh. 'But that's not reason enough to . . . well, I can't . . . You must see that I can't possible marry you.'

'Why on earth not?' he demanded.

She shrugged helplessly. 'There are so many reasons. There's the past, for instance. I'm sorry, Giles, but I'd never feel that I could really trust you. All those girl-friends of yours—like Melanie.' She grimaced. 'And what about Polly? I can't possibly leave the girl. I—well, I promised her father that . . .'

'Hang on!' Giles said firmly. 'Let's deal with one thing at a time—starting with the past, hmm?' He put an arm about her, and drew her close to his warm body. 'Since you came back to Eastdale, you've accused me, more than once, of lying to you. It's taken me some time to sort it all out—and it wasn't until I talked to Polly, when she told me your true age, that all the pieces of the puzzle came together.'

Alicia looked at him in astonishment. 'My—my true age . . .?'

'I now know that we've been the victim of other people's lies,' he sighed heavily. 'Of course, I should never have believed Jed. I might have known that stepfather of yours was out to make trouble.'

'Jed?'

'Oh, God—I was so in love with you,' Giles murmured, drawing her closer. 'I didn't know it at the time, of course. I only knew that you had become a fever in my blood, a sexual thirst that I could barely control. And yet you were so young, so innocent as you rode with me about the estate,' he whispered, burying his face in her fragrant blonde hair. 'It became harder and harder for me to restrain myself, and then we made love that day by the haystack. It all seemed so right, so beautiful. Nothing mattered, except that I knew I loved you, that I wanted to marry you, and that my feelings would last for ever. And then, two weeks later, Jed came to see me. After I'd been forced to listen to what he had to say, my whole world collapsed like a pack of cards.' He rubbed a hand over his eyes, as if trying to erase a painful memory.

'I don't understand.' Listening to his words, Alicia had been carried back in time to that hot summer when life, and love, had seemed so simple to comprehend. An idyllic Garden of Eden, before reality had broken through its flimsy portals, to bring aching unhappiness in its wake.

'Jed told me that you were only fifteen. He

informed me that if I ever saw you again, he'd report me to the police for interfering with a child under the age of consent,' said Giles bitterly.

'*No . . .!* You didn't . . . it's not true!'

'I know that now. But can you imagine how I felt at the time? Of course I knew that you'd been a virgin when I first made love to you, but I'd believed you when you said you were nearly eighteen. And there I was—a man who'd corrupted a young girl—practically a child! My God! I nearly went berserk!'

'But Jed was lying!' she protested earnestly. 'I mean, I know I added a year to my age, but . . .'

'But I didn't know that. It never occurred to me that Jed might not be telling the truth. Why should he lie?' Giles gestured helplessly.

'I don't know,' she said slowly. 'Maybe he was trying to look after me, in his own peculiar way. I know . . .' she said as he gave a harsh snort of derision. 'But he had warned me to keep away from you, and I think he honestly thought you were way out of my class and money bracket . . .'

'What nonsense!' Giles growled.

Alicia shrugged. 'Jed was furious when he found out about us, and locked me in my room. It took me almost a day to escape, and when I did manage to get to the Hall, Camilla said you were away on holiday.'

'*Holiday!*' He gave a harsh laugh. 'I honestly don't remember too clearly what I did after Jed had been to see me. I just got in the car and drove as far away from Shropshire as I could, ending up at a pub in Devon, where I stayed for a week, walking over the moors all day and getting paralytically drunk every night. By the time I sobered up and came back to Eastdale, it was too late. You'd disappeared from the face of the earth.'

'Apart from saying you were on holiday, Camilla told me that you and she were engaged, and that I

was only one of a crowd of silly young girls who'd
been fooled and seduced by you.'

'Oh, Alicia . . .' he groaned.

'I didn't stop to think,' she murmured sadly. 'I—
well, I just knew that I had to get away from the
farm, and you. So I ran away. I could have ended up
anywhere, but when I hitched a lift, the lorry driver
told me he was going to London.' She shrugged.
'Quite honestly, after what Camilla had said, I didn't
care what I did, or where I went.'

'Camilla!' he sighed heavily. 'I don't know what
she told you, but it had to be a pack of lies. I'll admit
that I'd had a brief affair with her, before I fell in
love with you. I suppose she must have wanted to
continue our liaison, but I was so blindingly enthralled
with your sweet body . . .' His fingers moved softly
over her skin, sending shivers of delight trembling
through her slim frame. 'Frankly, darling, I simply
wasn't aware of her existence. I remained friendly
with her—after all, our families had known each
other for years—and she'd call in for a drink
occasionally. But that was it. I certainly wasn't
engaged to her, far from it. Apart from the times
when you and I made love, my mind was solely
concerned with the question of how soon I could
decently get married to such a young girl. You see, I
knew I had to have you—to marry you. The only
problem seemed to be whether I was being unfair in
wanting to rush such a young girl to the altar.'

'Camilla . . . she was . . . well, she was very
convincing,' Alicia said quietly.

'I've been telling you the absolute truth,' he assured
her, and there was no mistaking the deep, genuine
note of sincerity in his voice. 'I did everything I could
to try and trace you after you'd gone—all to no avail.
I even tried the Salvation Army, but they couldn't
find you either. You could have been anywhere:
Birmingham, Manchester, London . . .' He fell silent,
his hands clenching at the agonising memories of so

long ao. 'And then I saw a picture in the paper—of you and your husband—and I read that you'd married a rich, elderly industrialist. God!—I was drunk for days after that. And then I didn't care what happened. Camilla seemed to be mad keen to marry me, and I didn't give a damn either way. So we got married, and lived unhappily every after!' he grated bitterly.

'Oh, Giles, I'm so sorry,' she whispered, putting her arms about him, and holding him close against her rapidly beating heart.

'Despite what she did to you, Camilla deserved a better fate than to be married to me. It was you, Alicia—and my continuing love for you—that was the real problem.' Giles sighed and gently kissed the soft mound of her breast. 'Of course, it wasn't really your fault, and it wasn't Camilla's fault, either—or only in so far as she'd made the mistake of wanting to marry me. It was hopeless. How on earth did I expect to live happily with the girl, when all I wanted was you? As you can imagine, our marriage was a disaster from day one—and we both knew it. I've never blamed Camilla for running off with Mark Wright, and I willingly gave her a divorce just as soon as I could.'

'And what about all the other women in your life?'

He gave a mock groan. 'Here we go again! Look, darling . . .' He sat up and lifted her face to his. 'I'm an ordinary, fairly red-blooded male, okay?' He possessed her lips in a lingering kiss. 'After my marriage ended so sourly, I left women strictly alone for a long time. However, it's been eight years since I fell in love with you, Alicia, and I'm not going to pretend that I've lived like a monk ever since. But there haven't been that many women, and *none* who ever touched my heart. I gave that to you a very long time ago, my dearest.'

'And Melanie Todd?' she smiled at him quizzically.

'Ah . . .' he grinned. 'She's extremely decorative— but please give me credit for knowing a predatory female when I see one! However, I was very encouraged to see just how jealous you were of her.'

'I wasn't!' she said indignantly.

'Liar! Anyway, what about you and Edmund Truscott? I know you've been out to dinner with him at least once—quite apart from any cosy little meetings you may have had about the damned tenancy business,' he growled. 'But in fact,' he hesitated for a moment, 'quite honestly, I've been far more worried about your late husband. You've obviously got so many memories, and he seems to have been a remarkable man . . .' Giles gave a heavy sigh.

Alicia put up a hand to softly touch his cheek. 'I loved Walter, but I was never *in love* with him. How could I be, when he wasn't you?' she said simply. 'I will always remember his kindness, his consideration and the home he gave me when I was so unhappy. I can't ever forget how good he was to me, and that's why . . .' she took a deep breath and swallowed hard, 'I—I can't marry you, Giles.' A hard lump seemed to be stuck in her throat, preventing her from saying any more.

'It's Polly, isn't it?' he said quietly, and when she nodded he clasped her tightly in his arms. 'I admire your resolution, but you're such an idiot, my love,' he whispered, gently stroking her hair. 'I can quite understand why he asked you to look after his daughter, but I'm sure your late husband wouldn't have wished you to sacrifice your own happiness to do so. However, Polly and I have discussed the matter, and we've sorted everything out between us.' He brushed his lips over her forehead.

'You and Polly? What are you talking about?'

'It cost me a fortune, but I had a long talk to her, yesterday, before flying back from Australia. I must say, that girl's a holy terror!' he laughed ruefully. 'She first of all wanted to know why I was so spineless, and I quote: "I'm sick and tired of all this

nonsense between you and Alicia—it's high time you
made an honest woman of my stepmother!"'

'Oh, no . . .' Alicia moaned, burying her flaming
cheeks in the curve of his shoulder.

'Oh, yes!' His body shook with laughter. 'When I
told her I would like nothing better, and asked
whether she had any helpful suggestions to offer, we
had a hard bargaining session before coming to an
amicable arrangement. In fact,' he smiled complacent-
ly. 'Polly has told me that she's looking forward to
being my stepdaughter. Although we're not quite
sure if that's the right description. Maybe it should be
step-stepdaughter . . .?' he added thoughtfully.

'You've got it all sorted out between you, haven't
you?' she retorted huffily. 'I don't suppose either of
you people thought of asking for *my* views on this
horrid little arrangement? Well, it just so happens . . .'

His mouth claimed hers in a passionate kiss that
seemed to last for ever. When at last he let her go,
she lay flushed and breathless in his arms. 'It just so
happens that after church, on the Sunday when you
were so busy trying to clean up Winterfloods, I had a
long talk with Mr Ellis. He told me that since you're
a widow, and taking into account the facts of my first
marriage, he'd be pleased to marry us in the village
church. Polly is insisting on being a bridesmaid, and
all I've got to do is to get hold of a special licence.
Therefore—my dearest love—if you don't agree to
my "horrid arrangements", I shall be left standing at
the altar. What a scandal! Just think what Mrs Jenkins
will have to say about that!'

'But I can't . . . there are all the problems over the
farm, and the tenancy, and . . .'

'I said that Polly and I came to an arrangement,
and so we have. Incidentaly, I wasn't lying the other
day. I do look after the Hall Farm myself, but with
four thousand acres and many tenant farmers on the
estate, I leave the matter of rents and tenancy
agreements to my land agents. I like to think that I

get on well with my tenants, and if they want to argue the toss about rents, etc, it's far better for them to fight it out with the agents than with myself. So Smith, Garratt and Robinson just naturally got on with what they saw as their job.' Giles sighed and pushed a hand roughly through his dark hair. 'Giving you—or anyone, for that matter—three weeks to leave their home was quite disgraceful. I've therefore decided to sack "Sue, Grabbit and Runne"—as you and Polly call them!—and Edmund Truscott is going to look after my affairs from now on.'

'But you still haven't answered my question. What about Winterfloods Farm?'

He grinned down at her. 'Oh, didn't I tell you? I'm giving the tenancy to Polly. We've agreed that she's to have a foreman running the place for her, while she goes to Cirencester Agricultural College—and learns to farm properly! So, if you don't marry me—I'm sorry to say that it looks as if you're going to be homeless.' He shook his head sorrowfully. 'Poor Alicia, it's all very sad!'

'Oh, shut up!' Alicia glared at him, not knowing whether to laugh or cry. 'Ever since I returned to Shropshire, people have been interfering with my life. There was Elsie and Mrs Renshaw conspiring together—you've no idea of what they've been up to!'

'Oh, yes I have!' he laughed. 'It took me long enough to get the idea into their thick heads. I must have spent hours dropping heavy hints, not to mention the long sessions in the kitchen with Mrs Renshaw, telling her how much I missed you . . .!'

'Why, you—you . . .' she gasped, beating her fists against his hard chest, and swearing furiously until he laughingly captured her hands, his body pressing her firmly down on the soft mattress. And then his hungry mouth was consuming hers in a kiss of devastating intensity, the liquid heat of desire flaring through her veins as she moaned and writhed beneath the hard arousal of his body.

'All's fair in love, my dearest,' he whispered, his mouth tracing an erotic path over her silky skin. 'And I intend to keep you imprisoned here, making mad passionate love to you, until you finally agree to marry me!'

A smiled tugged at the corner of Alicia's mouth. 'Is that a firm promise? Because if so, I don't think I'm going to be in too much of a hurry to make up my mind!' she teased, before sighing with content as she abandoned herself to the possession of her future husband.

YOU'RE INVITED TO ACCEPT **FOUR ROMANCES** AND A TOTE BAG **FREE!**

Acceptance card

| NO STAMP NEEDED | **Post to: Reader Service, FREEPOST, P.O. Box 236, Croydon, Surrey. CR9 9EL** |

Please note readers in Southern Africa write to:
Independant Book Services P.T.Y., Postbag X3010, Randburg 2125, S. Africa

YES! Please send me 4 free Mills & Boon Romances and my free tote bag – and reserve a Reader Service Subscription for me. If I decide to subscribe I shall receive 6 new Romances every month as soon as they come off the presses for £7.20 together with a FREE monthly newsletter including information on top authors and special offers, exclusively for Reader Service subscribers. There are no postage and packing charges, and I understand I may cancel or suspend my subscription at any time. If I decide not to subscribe I shall write to you within 10 days. Even if I decide not to subscribe the 4 free novels and the tote bag are mine to keep forever. I am over 18 years of age   EP20R

NAME _____

(CAPITALS PLEASE)

ADDRESS _____

_____

_____ **POSTCODE** _____

ROMANCE

Variety is the spice of romance

Each month, Mills & Boon publish new romances. New stories about people falling in love. A world of variety in romance — from the best writers in the romantic world. Choose from these titles in May.

THE SHADOW OF MOONLIGHT Lindsay Armstrong
DREAM OF LOVE Kay Clifford
SINGLE COMBAT Sandra Field
FANTASY UNLIMITED Claire Harrison
THE EAGLE AND THE SUN Dana James
A SAVAGE ADORATION Penny Jordan
CIRCLE OF FATE Charlotte Lamb
HAY FEVER Mary Lyons
TOUCH AND GO Elizabeth Oldfield
BROKEN SILENCE Kate Walker
*A DANGEROUS PASSION Jayne Bauling
*NO STRINGS ATTACHED Annabel Murray

On sale where you buy paperbacks. If you require further information or have any difficulty obtaining them, write to: Mills & Boon Reader Service, PO Box 236, Thornton Road, Croydon, Surrey CR9 3RU, England.

*These two titles are available *only* from Mills & Boon Reader Service.

Mills & Boon
the rose of romance

ROMANCE